MARC'S MISSION

ALSO BY JOCKO WILLINK

Way of the Warrior Kid: From Wimpy
to Warrior the Navy SEAL Way

WAY of the WARRIOR KID MARC'S MISSION

JOCKO WILLINK

ILLUSTRATED BY JON BOZAK

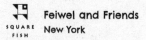
Feiwel and Friends
New York

SQUARE
FISH

An imprint of Macmillan Publishing Group, LLC
175 Fifth Avenue, New York, NY 10010
mackids.com

Library of Congress Control Number: 2017944823

ISBN 978-1-250-29443-2 (paperback)   ISBN 978-1-250-15680-8 (ebook)

Originally published in the United States by Feiwel and Friends
First Square Fish edition, 2019
Book designed by Sophie Erb
Square Fish logo designed by Filomena Tuosto

10 9 8 7 6 5 4 3 2 1

AR: 4.0

This book is dedicated to the men of SEAL Team Three,

Task Unit Bruiser.

Especially:

Marc Lee, Mike Monsoor, and Ryan Job,

who lived, and fought, and died

as warriors.

Chris Kyle, whose legend was larger than life,

but not as big as his heart.

And Seth Stone,

who never let me down.

Ever.

MARC'S MISSION

The Warrior Kid Code

1. The Warrior Kid wakes up early in the morning.
2. The Warrior Kid studies to learn and gain knowledge and asks questions if he doesn't understand.
3. The Warrior Kid trains hard, exercises, and eats right to be strong and fast and healthy.
4. The Warrior Kid trains to know how to fight so he can stand up to bullies to protect the weak.
5. The Warrior Kid treats people with respect and helps out other people whenever possible.
6. The Warrior Kid keeps things neat and is always prepared and ready for action.
7. The Warrior Kid stays humble.
8. The Warrior Kid works hard and always does his best.
9. I am the Warrior Kid.

CHAPTER 1: THE PUMPKIN AND THE PRINCIPAL

This year was a really good year—until the last day of school. I ended up in a place I NEVER SHOULD HAVE BEEN: THE PRINCIPAL'S OFFICE! Yes, that's right. Me, Mr. Warrior Kid with my Warrior Code got sent to the principal's office! What for, you wonder?

Let me tell you in one word: NATHAN. That's right. I got sent to the principal's office because of Nathan James— a guy with two first names!

Here is the thing with Nathan: He is SUPER ANNOYING. He's always moving. Tapping. Snapping. Shifting. Bouncing his leg. Standing up. Sitting down. He just never stops moving. It is SO ANNOYING.

He is also always making comments and saying things to me and the other kids. Not exactly nice things, either. He calls us names. Mean names. He calls Kenny Williamson "Blockhead." He calls Patricia Johnson "Needle Nose." And he calls me "Plate Face." I don't know why. I don't think I look like a plate!

Okay, maybe my face is a little round, but that doesn't make it okay to call me Plate Face.

And the thing about Nathan is that he says it kind of jokingly but at the same time kind of seriously. So if we told on him, we would seem like tattletales.

Today, we were helping clean the classroom. Some kids were taking down pictures, some kids were clearing out desks, some kids were counting and stacking books. I got put in the group with Nathan, cleaning the art area.

He started in on me right away. "Let's get this cleaned up, Plate Face."

"Don't call me that," I told him.

"Don't call you what, Plate Face?"

"Plate Face."

"I know you're Plate Face," he said.

I started to raise my voice. "Don't call me that!" I felt my face turning red because I was SO ANNOYED.

"Well, what do you want me to call you?" he said.

"Call me by my name," I answered. I looked at Nathan, and he looked a little scared.

"Okay, fine," he said. I think he realized that he had pushed too far and knew what might happen.

Then he whispered, "Plate Face," and smiled.

I felt my hands clench together. I bit down hard, squeezed my jaw, and started to breathe hard. The more I stood there and thought about it, the madder I got. When Nathan saw that I was getting mad, his smile grew even more. I could feel my face turning redder and redder by the second. Then Nathan chuckled a little bit. He was laughing at my anger! I got so mad that I wanted to explode or scream or throw something at him.

PLATE FACE

That's when I noticed a bright-orange papier-mâché pumpkin that one of my classmates had made in art sitting right in front of me. It was about the size of a volleyball—and it looked perfect. Without thinking, I grabbed the pumpkin and threw it right at Nathan's head really, really hard. He wasn't expecting it at all, so

it hit him square in the face. It hit him so hard that he tripped over a stuffed caterpillar and fell to the ground, knocking over an easel on his way down. It made a GI-ANT noise, and everyone looked over at us.

This is where it got REALLY BAD. The pumpkin ricocheted off Nathan's head and made a straight shot at our teacher, Ms. Carpenter. Right as she looked to see what the big noise was, it hit her: POW!! RIGHT IN THE FACE! Luckily, it was only papier-mâché, so it didn't hurt her in any way. But it did make her stumble back into her desk and spill her coffee. I had never seen Ms. Carpenter get mad before. And I hope I never see it again. She turned bright red and looked like she was ready to KILL ME!

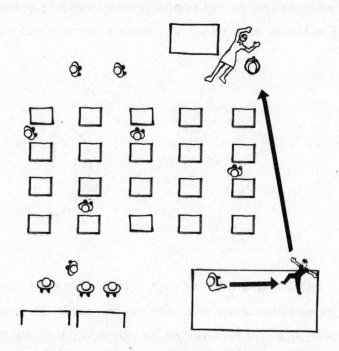

But instead, her voice got really, really quiet, like a low growl from a crazed animal, and she grumbled, "GET. TO. THE. PRINCIPAL'S. OFFICE. NOW."

I quickly made my way to Principal Forrest's office, and as I did, tears started to roll down my face. I couldn't believe it! It was my last day of school and I was getting sent to the principal's office!

Once I got to the principal's office, his secretary told me to sit down outside his office. I guess I had cried enough, because I started to calm down. Ms. Carpenter walked in a minute later, went straight into Principal Forrest's office without even looking at me, and shut the door behind her.

A few minutes later, she walked out and stopped in front of me. She didn't look that mad anymore. After a few seconds, she said, "I'm disappointed, Marc. Very disappointed."

I started to say something back to her. "But . . . I . . . it was . . ." But she walked away.

Then Principal Forrest called out, "Come on into my office, Marc."

I walked into his office with my head hung low.

"Well?" he said.

"I'm sorry. I just . . . I got . . . it was . . . it was Nathan. He keeps calling me Plate Face. And he has been calling me that the whole year. And today he just kept saying it over and over and over again, even when I asked him not to!"

"And you think that gives you the right to try to hurt him? And to hurt Ms. Carpenter?"

"No, but–"

"Exactly, Marc. NO BUTS. I'm sending you home from

school. I'm calling your parents at home to come pick you up."

My heart sank. I couldn't believe this. My mom and dad were going to ground me for the rest of my natural life! Then I realized I might be okay. My dad had gone overseas for his job building a factory; he'd left two weeks ago. He would be gone for the whole summer. Also, my

Marc,
Blah, blah, blah, you're in trouble. Blah, blah, blah, lots of trouble. Blah, blah, trouble, trouble, trouble.

mom had recently started a new job. . . . Well, not a totally new job, but a new job at the same place. She got promoted and is now in charge of a bunch of stuff, so she is working a ton now. Most of the time she doesn't get home until well after dinner. Sometimes she even gets home after I'm asleep. So there was no way she would be home today—which was good—because that meant she wouldn't be there to answer this call, and by the time she did get home, school would be over. I was saved!

Principal Forrest's secretary brought in a piece of paper with my home phone number on it. He dialed the number. I knew no one would answer, but I sat patiently. Then, all of a sudden, Principal Forrest spoke. "Hello, I'm looking for Marc's mom or dad?" There was a pause as he listened. "Oh, that's fine. Are either his mom or dad home?"

Who could he be talking to? I thought to myself.

"Oh. Okay. Well, let me tell you the situation: Marc had an outburst in school today. He ended up throwing an object at another student, and it hit both the student and his teacher. I'm sending him home from school so he can think about his behavior. Can you come pick him up?"

I still had no idea who he was talking to.

"Okay. Great. We'll see you in a few minutes. Thank you."

The principal hung up the phone, then looked at me.

"You're going home. Your uncle is coming to pick you up."

I remembered instantly: Uncle Jake had arrived today while I was at school! My mom had invited him to stay with us over the summer and help keep track of me since my dad was gone and she was so busy at work. She had left a key under the mat by the door, and Uncle Jake was at my house, and now he was coming to get me! And he was going to know EVERYTHING.

I started to cry. And it wasn't just because of Nathan or being sent to the principal's office or being sent home from school or even having Uncle Jake know how much trouble I had caused. There were a bunch of other things that were going to make this the worst summer ever. And it was just starting.

CHAPTER 2: APOLOGIES

I was sitting on the bench just outside the principal's office, crying like a little baby. I couldn't believe that this was happening, and I kept whispering to myself over and over again, "I am so stupid. I am so stupid."

It was Uncle Jake's first day in town for summer vacation and he was picking me up from THE PRINCIPAL'S OFFICE! He did so much for me last summer. He taught me how to swim and how to study, he got me into jiu-jitsu, and he also put me on a good workout program so I could actually do pull-ups. He turned me from a wimpy kid to a Warrior Kid, and this is how I pay him back?!?! By getting in trouble and getting sent home from school?!?!

The more I thought about it, the more I knew how badly I had let him down—and the worse I felt. On top of all that, what kind of punishment was I about to get? Was I going to be grounded for the whole summer? Longer? Maybe until Christmas? Would I even be allowed to celebrate Christmas anymore? And Uncle Jake—was he even going to talk to me now that I had done this?

I put my head in my hands and sat there, crying. Then I heard a familiar voice. "How ya doin', Marc?"

I looked up.

It was Uncle Jake. He didn't even look mad. He didn't look upset. He just looked, well, kind of normal, I guess. But I didn't feel too normal.

"Not good, Uncle Jake. Not good," I told him, tears running down my face.

"All right. Well. Let's get you out of here and then you can tell me what's going on."

Uncle Jake stepped into the principal's office and shut the door. I could hear them talking, but I couldn't hear what they were saying. A couple of minutes later, Uncle Jake walked out.

"Come on," Uncle Jake said. "Take me to Ms. Carpenter's room."

"But I'm supposed to go home," I told him.

"Not until you say sorry to Ms. Carpenter and Nathan."

"But I got kicked out–"

"The principal called the classroom. Nathan and Ms. Carpenter will be waiting outside."

"But Nathan is the whole reason this happened," I protested.

"No, he's not. You can't blame other people for the things that *you* do. You are the reason. You lost your temper. You lost control. Because of that, you made a bad decision. Now you are going to apologize, and you better mean it. Then I will take you home. Got it?"

"Yes, Uncle Jake, I got it."

As soon as we turned the corner down the hallway, I could see Ms. Carpenter and Nathan standing alone outside the classroom. I held my head down in shame. When we got close enough, we stopped in front of them.

"Go ahead," Uncle Jake said.

I looked up at Ms. Carpenter. I felt horrible. I really was sorry that I hit her with the pumpkin, so I told her that. "I'm sorry, Ms. Carpenter."

"Okay, Marc. I am really disappointed, but I accept your apology. Don't let it happen again."

"I won't, Ms. Carpenter. I promise." Then I glanced at Nathan. He had a little smirk on his face. I didn't want to say I was sorry to him—why would I? He was the whole reason I was there!!

"And?" said Uncle Jake.

I stood there. This was AWFUL! I had to either apologize to my worst enemy for something *he* made me do, or not do what my uncle Jake—the best uncle in the world—was telling me to do.

Uncle Jake followed up sternly, "Marc. Go ahead and apologize."

This was one of those situations where I realized Uncle Jake was going to get me to do what he wanted me to do WHETHER I LIKED IT OR NOT!

So I swallowed hard, looked at the ground, and mumbled, "I'm sorry."

I'll just have to be the bigger man here.

"What?" said Uncle Jake. "Louder."

There was no getting around this. And I figured I was in big enough trouble anyway. So I took a deep breath, looked Nathan in the eyes, and said, "I'm sorry, Nathan."

Nathan's smirk turned into a smile, and he said, "I bet you are—"

He'd barely finished those words when Ms. Carpenter cut him off quickly. "Nathan James, you cut it with that attitude and accept Marc's apology. NOW."

He knew he could get in trouble, too, so he stepped back, looked up at me, and said, "Apology accepted, Marc." It didn't sound very convincing, but it was enough for Ms. Carpenter, who then put her arm around Nathan, thanked Uncle Jake, and guided Nathan back into the classroom.

Once Nathan was in the classroom, Ms. Carpenter bent down and looked me in the eyes. "You are better than that, Marc. At least, you should be." She looked really disappointed in me, and I felt like I'd really let her down. Then she turned, walked into the classroom, and shut the door.

"Come on, Marc," Uncle Jake said as he spun around and headed toward the exit. "Let's get you out of here."

We walked down the corridor, out the door, through the courtyard, and into the parking lot without saying a word. I didn't think Uncle Jake would ever talk to me again. This summer was getting worse by the minute!

CHAPTER 3: THE MIRROR

I walked slowly to the car and got in. Uncle Jake started the car and began driving. Then he said quietly, "So what happened, Marc?"

Uncle Jake's voice kind of calmed me down. I thought he would be mad at me, but instead it seemed like he was just trying to understand what happened.

"I threw a papier-mâché pumpkin at Nathan James. It hit him in the face, then it hit Ms. Carpenter in the face."

Uncle Jake kind of smiled—I didn't expect that—and then he said, "I know that part, Marc. The principal already told me. What I'm asking is why did that happen? Why did you do it?"

"Because Nathan is annoying! Really annoying!"

"So do you throw a papier-mâché pumpkin at every person that annoys you?" he asked.

"No. I don't," I said back.

"Then what made you do it this time?"

"He kept calling me Plate Face!"

"Plate Face?"

"Yes! Plate Face."

Uncle Jake laughed. HE LAUGHED!

"It's not funny!" I told him.

"It's kind of funny," he said.

"I DON'T LOOK LIKE A PLATE!" I told Uncle Jake.

"You do have a pretty round face," Uncle Jake said.

"NO I DON'T!" I told him. And when I told him this, I have to admit . . . I was kind of yelling. I was really mad. REALLY MAD.

"Rounder than most faces, I mean. You've seen your face, right? In a mirror?" Uncle Jake asked me, still laughing a little bit. I couldn't believe this! Uncle Jake was agreeing with Nathan James and saying I ACTUALLY

I wouldn't call it a plate face. Maybe a handsome plate face . . . ?

WAS A PLATE FACE. Tears started to flow down my face again. I could feel my blood begin to boil.

"YES, I'VE SEEN MY FACE IN A MIRROR BEFORE, AND I DON'T LOOK LIKE A PLATE!" I yelled. I couldn't stop myself from screaming. It was like the whole world was against me—even my hero, Uncle Jake.

Suddenly, Uncle Jake pulled the car over to the side of the road, put it into PARK, and said, "Look at your face right now and tell me what you see." Then he flipped down the visor of the car and pointed the mirror at my face.

I looked in the mirror. "I don't see a plate face!" I barked at Uncle Jake.

"Okay. Then what *do* you see?" he asked.

I sat and looked at myself. My face didn't look like a plate, but it *was* bright red. My cheeks were covered in tears. My nose even had slime running out of it!

"What do you see? Really. Look at yourself and tell me what you see," Uncle Jake asked again.

I looked at myself. The tears. The runny nose. The red face. I knew exactly what I looked like. So I told Uncle Jake.

"A baby. I look like a big baby."

Uncle Jake smiled and nodded. "And why do you think you look like a big baby?"

I knew exactly where Uncle Jake was going with that question. And I knew exactly what the answer was. So I told him. "Because I'm acting like one?"

Uncle Jake nodded his head. "I'd say that is a pretty good answer. What does a baby act like?"

"Well, they get mad and frustrated and they scream and cry and throw things."

"Ah . . . yes. They get frustrated and they scream and cry and throw things. That sounds familiar," Uncle Jake said with a knowing look on his face. "But do you know why they do that?"

"Because they get mad or frustrated?"

"But everyone gets mad and frustrated. Those are called emotions. Anger. Sadness. Frustration. And there are good emotions, too, like happiness and excitement.

But here is the thing: Babies can't control their emotions. They don't know how. So they scream and cry. And that's what you just did. You acted like a baby. Warriors have to keep control over their emotions. Especially over something as silly as someone calling you a name."

HAPPINESS   FRUSTRATION

"Well . . ." I realized there were a lot of other things I needed to tell Uncle Jake. You see, it wasn't just Nathan James who was making me frustrated. There were a bunch of things that had been bothering me, and I was just starting to realize it. But I didn't know how to tell Uncle Jake.

"'Well' what?" Uncle Jake asked.

"I . . . I just . . ." I didn't know how to explain every-thing in a way that would make sense.

"You 'just' what?"

"There are some other things that are bothering me, too."

"Like what?" Uncle Jake asked. I wondered if I should tell Uncle Jake, but I figured that since he helped me last summer, maybe he could help me this summer, too. "Just tell me," Uncle Jake said.

"Okay, here goes. The first thing that is bothering me is this summer. I was ready for a nice summer, a break from school, hanging out with my friends, and being able to do some workouts with you. But a bunch of things happened, and now it seems like summer is ruined. First of all, I have to go to a dumb camp this summer. Only it isn't even a camp, and it isn't even camping. It's just in the recreation center, and we're supposed to be doing physical education and also reviewing math and spelling and a bunch of other school stuff. So it's basically school in the summertime! And if that isn't bad enough, it turns out that Nathan James is doing it, too! The one kid I despise! It would be a little better if I had a new bike to get there. But my mom won't get me a new bike. I even took her to the bike shop to see the best bike ever—The Bentlee. I thought maybe when she saw it in all its beauty, she would get it for me. NOPE! She has no soul!"

"So that's it? The camp and a bike and that's why you think this summer will be awful? Because you have to go to camp and your mom won't buy you a new bike?"

There's no way my summer doesn't get better with a Bentlee!!

There was one more thing, only I was very afraid to tell Uncle Jake about it. But, once again, I figured that if I didn't tell him, then he couldn't help me. So I told him.

"It's jiu-jitsu."

"Jiu-jitsu? I thought you liked jiu-jitsu?"

"I do. I have fun at jiu-jitsu and I really like it."

"So what's the problem?" asked Uncle Jake.

"The problem is that my coach wants me to compete in a tournament."

"Why is that a problem?"

"Because I don't want to."

"Why?"

"Because."

"'Because'?"

"Yes, Uncle Jake, *because*. Just because. I don't want to."

Uncle Jake sat for a minute, quietly. Then he said, "So. You have to go to camp. You don't like Nathan. You want a new bike. And you need to compete in jiu-jitsu. Those are the problems that you think will ruin your summer?"

"I don't *think* they will ruin my summer—THEY ALREADY ARE RUINING MY SUMMER! LOOK AT ME!" I pointed at myself in the mirror. I wasn't crying anymore, but you could still tell that I was upset.

Uncle Jake nodded and then sat quietly for a minute. "Well," he finally said, "do you remember all the problems you overcame last summer?"

"Of course I do, Uncle Jake."

"Well, these are all problems that many people have. And these are problems you can overcome, too. But they are not going to be easy to overcome. In order to overcome these problems, you are going to have to use what you already know about being a Warrior Kid—but you are going to have to do even more. It will be hard work. And it will test you in different ways than pull-ups and swimming and studying did. These will test your mind, your emotions, and your discipline. But if you pass the test, these problems will be solved, and this will be the best summer ever. Are you willing to be put to the test, Marc?"

I quickly remembered the early wake-ups, lots of studying, and crazy exercising I did the last time Uncle Jake helped me solve my problems. But I also remembered overcoming all those problems and becoming faster, stronger, and smarter than I was before. And that felt GOOD!

"Yes, Uncle Jake. I am ready. And I am willing."

"Okay, then, Marc. Let's head home. We will go from there."

Uncle Jake got that strange smile on his face that I hadn't seen since he left. It looked like he was going to enjoy this. I just wasn't sure I would feel the same way!

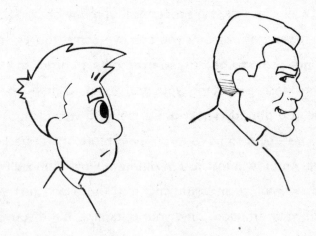

CHAPTER 4: MY PROBLEMS

Uncle Jake is definitely back for the summer! He woke me up this morning at zero dark thirty and we went down to the garage and did a workout. I must admit, it is a lot more fun working out with Uncle Jake now that I am stronger. We did pull-ups, push-ups, sit-ups, and jumping jacks. Even though I wasn't doing as many of the exercises as Uncle Jake, he still told me I did a good job.

That made me feel awesome, because I worked out through the whole school year. I stayed a Warrior Kid for almost the whole school year. I say *almost* because there were some days when I was too tired or too busy to work out, so I skipped a day or two. But my rule was to never ever miss three days in a row of working out, and I didn't.

My eating was pretty good, too. Although, there was a time when my mom and dad were working a lot and getting home late every night. I have to admit that I had mint chocolate chip ice cream for dinner three nights in a row. OOPS! But also MMMMMMMM! After that third day, I didn't eat dessert for two weeks!

Once we finished our workout, we got changed and sat down for some breakfast. Uncle Jake told me that he'd told my mom about me being sent to the principal's office and then home from school. I figured that was it! My summer was OVER!

"What did she say?" I asked him, expecting the worst.

"She wasn't happy. She wanted to ground you. For a long time. But I told her I would take care of it. So you owe me."

"Thanks," I said but then I wondered what that meant, so I asked him. "Wait. What do I owe you?"

"Well. I told her about some of these problems you're having. And I told her I would make sure they got fixed."

Yes! I thought to myself. *Now I am set! Uncle Jake is going to fix everything. He will get me out of that stupid camp, teach me how to deal with Nathan, get me out of the jiu-jitsu tournament, and buy me a new bike!* "Thanks, Uncle Jake!" I said. "I knew you would fix everything!"

But he didn't say "You're welcome" or "No problem" or anything. Instead he just sat there and looked at me. Then after a minute he said, "*I'm* not going to fix anything. YOU are."

I should have known there would be a catch! And I was right–there it was, and it didn't make any sense.

"Uncle Jake, I can't fix these problems. Nathan is mean, and there is nothing I can do about that. My mom already signed me up for the camp, and she said I have to go. And I can't get a new bike because I have no money. And my jiu-jitsu instructor is making me do the tournament! So even though I would love to solve these problems, I can't, because the problems aren't mine!"

Uncle Jake listened and nodded his head as if he already knew everything I was saying. Then he spoke. "Actually, the problems are yours. In fact, *you* are the problem. We aren't going to change the problems. We are going to change your attitude."

This made no sense to me at all. These problems weren't my fault. I didn't have any idea how my attitude was going to change them. So I asked Uncle Jake very bluntly, "How can my attitude get me a new bike? How can my attitude get me out of summer camp? How can my attitude make Nathan a nice person? And how can my attitude get me out of the jiu-jitsu tournament?"

Uncle Jake took a breath before he spoke. "Well, Marc. Your attitude actually changes everything. Especially things that you don't think you can change. Look at how you are blaming everyone else for your problems. If you don't think the problems are yours, how can you solve them?"

"But how can—" I started to say.

"You can't. If you think that every problem you have is someone else's, then how can you ever get them fixed? By sitting around and waiting for other people to change or waiting for other people to act? You might be waiting for a really long time. But if you look at a problem from a different perspective—a perspective where the problem is actually your fault—then you can do something to fix it."

"Yeah, but sometimes there is really nothing I can do. Nothing! Like summer camp. I'm going. My mom said there was no question about it. But I don't want to. AT ALL!"

"Okay, then. You know it is definitely going to happen. So we will look at your attitude toward summer camp and go from there."

"I think it's pretty clear what my attitude is—I don't want to go!" I told Uncle Jake, my voice getting louder.

"I get that. And I also see that you're getting emotional again. So calm down. If you are getting emotional, then you have to recognize that and start to calm yourself down. Warriors don't lose their tempers. So get yours under control. Take a breath. Think about something else. Think about something more important than this little summer camp."

"It's not little to me! It's my whole summer!" I told Uncle Jake, trying to stay calm but not really doing a good job of it.

"I get that. I get that all these things seem like big, horrible problems to you. And that's okay. I get it. But warriors have to deal with problems all the time on the battlefield. And they can't just sit around and wait for someone else to fix them. *They* have to fix the problems themselves. And *you* have to fix these problems, because no one else is going to fix them for you. And the number-one thing you are going to do to get these problems fixed is fix your attitude. Understand?"

I didn't know what to say because I actually didn't understand. So I told him, "Not really."

"Well, you will understand, Marc. You will."

CHAPTER 5: EARN IT

I'm starting to understand what Uncle Jake meant about my attitude—and I'm starting to understand that I have the wrong attitude about a lot of things.

Of course, even though it was Sunday, the day started with a workout. Again, it was a really good workout. And even though I have become stronger, I still have a LONG WAY TO GO to be as strong as Uncle Jake. He brought up last summer and asked me if I remembered doing one hundred pull-ups. Of course I did! I didn't do them in a row, but I did them.

"How long do you think it took you to do one hundred pull-ups?" Uncle Jake asked.

"I don't know. Maybe forty-five minutes. Or an hour. I know I needed to rest a bunch."

Uncle Jake pointed to my watch. "Get ready to time me," he said. I put my watch into stopwatch mode.

"Ready," I told him.

"Set, GO!" he said. With that, he jumped up onto the pull-up bar. I was counting one, two, three, four, five, six, seven, eight, nine, ten . . . He didn't even look fazed. . . . Twenty-two, twenty-three, twenty-four, twenty-five . . . He still didn't even slow down. . . . Thirty-six, thirty-seven, thirty-eight . . . Uncle Jake was like a pull-up machine! He kept going. . . . Forty-eight, forty-nine, fifty, fifty-one, fifty-two . . . He took a pause right before fifty-three, then did seven more and got to sixty. IN ONE SET! Then he shook his arms a bit, jumped back on the bar, and did another twenty, getting all the way to eighty. He jumped on the bar for eighty-one, eighty-two, eighty-three . . . He dropped off the bar at ninety-three, then jumped back up and did

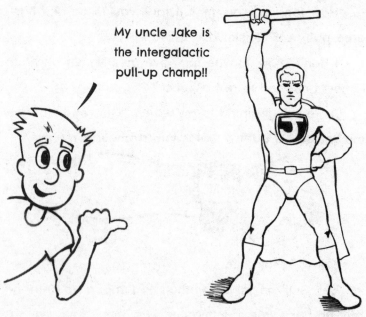

My uncle Jake is the intergalactic pull-up champ!!

his last seven for a total of one hundred. As soon as he finished, he dropped off the bar, looked at me, and shouted, "Time!" I pressed STOP on the stopwatch.

"How'd I do?" he asked.

"Four minutes and thirty-four seconds," I told him.

"Roger that. Not too bad."

"'Not too bad'?" I replied. "That's crazy! It took me forty-five minutes."

"But I can do better. I need to keep working hard," he told me.

"I guess I need to keep working hard, too," I said.

"We all do," he replied. He paused for a moment before speaking again. "So what's going on with the bike that you want so bad?"

"The Bentlee? Oh, it is AWESOME," I told him.

"What makes it so awesome?" he asked.

"EVERYTHING," I told him. "It's got a super comfy seat, sweet handlebars, and it's all shiny silver with gold rims."

"Gold, huh?" Uncle Jake said.

"Yeah, super shiny . . ." I was excited, but the look on Uncle Jake's face made me think maybe I shouldn't be so excited about it.

"Okay. So you want a super shiny Bentlee, but what about the bike that you have right now?"

"That old bike? Oh, that bike is JUNK!" I told him.

"Where is it?" he asked.

"Outside by the shed," I told him.

"Well, go get it. I want to have a look."

I walked out of the garage, where we were working out, and over to the shed, then grabbed my old junky bike that was leaning against the shed and brought it back to the garage. "Bring it in," said Uncle Jake. So I brought the old rust bucket right into the garage. Once in there, I tried to put down the kickstand, but it wouldn't budge, so I laid the bike down on the ground. I stepped back and had a look. The tires were flat. The rims were rusty. One of the pedals was broken in half. One of the grips was all tattered and about to fall off. The seat was twisted and worn, and the frame of the bike itself had spots of rust all over it.

"Junk," I said to Uncle Jake.

"You think so?"

"Yeah! Look at it!"

"I am looking at it. How long have you had it?"

"Two years."

"And your mom doesn't think you need a new one?" he asked.

This is where things got kind of tricky. And this is where I started to realize MY attitude was not good. "Well," I told him, "not exactly."

"What do you mean 'not exactly'?"

Yep. Like I said. This is where I had some explaining to do. "I mean, my mom knows I need a new bike. But she won't get me one. She says I don't deserve it."

"She said you don't deserve it? Why not?"

"Because of this," I said shamefully as I pointed at my old, rusty, piece-of-junk bike. "She said I didn't take care of it."

Uncle Jake laughed. "I have to agree with your mom! It doesn't look like you took care of this at all! If you take care of a bike properly, it can last forever. But if you don't take care of it . . . well, this is what you get," Uncle Jake said as he pointed at my old, rusty bike. Then he looked back at me, got very serious, and said, "In the SEAL Teams, we have a saying: 'Take care of your gear and your gear will take care of you.' We applied that to every piece of gear we used. Our parachutes. Our scuba equipment. Our weapons. Our radios. Not just our personal gear, either. Our boats and motors. Our vehi-cles. Everything. You know what happens if you don't take care of your parachute?"

I was pretty sure I knew the answer to that question, but before I could get it out of my mouth, Uncle Jake answered: "You die. And it's the same with your scuba gear. If it fails, you die. Our weapons. Our radios. Our boats and motors and vehicles. All of it. If we don't take care of our gear, it could cost us our lives. So we take care of our gear—all the time, every time. WE TAKE CARE OF OUR GEAR. But it looks like you didn't. So your mom

is right. She would be silly to spend her hard-earned money on gear for you. You don't take care of your gear. You don't deserve a new bike."

I didn't know what to say, because, obviously, Uncle Jake was RIGHT! I hadn't taken care of the bike the way I should have. That is why it was in such bad condition. The thing was, even though I knew I was wrong, I still wanted a new bike—and I actually needed a new bike since this one was a disaster!

And I had an idea.

"But I still need a new bike. So maybe if I explain to my mom that I will take care of it, she will buy me one." This seemed like a good idea to me.

"Really?" Uncle Jake said in a voice that made me think maybe it wasn't such a good idea. "How much does this new bike cost?" he asked me.

"The Bentlee bike costs one hundred eighty-nine dollars," I told him.

"One hundred eighty-nine dollars?" he said with a look of surprise on his face. "That's a lot of money. Especially for a kid who already wasted a bunch of money letting *this* bike get ruined."

"It's not that much money for my mom," I told him, figuring that, since my mom has a car and a house and other stuff that costs way more than one hundred eighty-nine dollars, that much money couldn't be *that* important to her.

When those words came out of my mouth, Uncle Jake didn't look happy. Then he shook his head, as if he was REALLY disappointed in what I just said.

"One hundred eighty-nine dollars is definitely a lot of money. Ten dollars is a lot of money. In fact, one dollar is a lot of money when you actually have to earn it, like your mom does. You don't work for your money, so maybe it doesn't seem like much to you." Then Uncle Jake got a look on his face, the kind of look that makes me a little nervous. "Let me ask you this," he said. "How bad do you want that Bentlee bike?"

YES! I thought to myself. *Uncle Jake is going to get me the bike!* He is the best! "I really want it—bad! It would be so awesome to have! It is the coolest bike ever, and if I got it, that would be the best thing in the world!" I told him all this just to seal the deal and make sure he would get it for me!

"Okay," he said. There was a long pause after he said this. Part of my mind thought that "Okay" meant "Okay, I'll get this bike for you, young Marc, because you are such a great kid!" But part of me thought he might have more to say—and it wasn't going to be what I wanted to hear. And that part turned out to be correct. He did have more to say, and it wasn't what I wanted to hear. "Then you will have to earn it."

"'Earn it'?" I said.

"Yes. Earn it. You see, you don't even really under-stand what that means. As a kid, your parents pretty

41

much give you everything. Your food. Your clothes. Your bed. The roof over your head. Even this rusty bike right here. And when you are given things for free, you don't appreciate their *value*—what they're worth. You don't appreciate that someone worked hard to get the money to buy you that bike. When you don't appreciate something, you don't take care of it. That's what happened with this bike here. Right?"

FREE VS. EARNED

Uncle Jake was correct. I hadn't ever really thought about that. "Yes, Uncle Jake. That's what happened."

"Okay, then. So if you want that new Bentlee bike, *you* are going to earn it. Understand?"

I thought about this for a second—and realized I didn't understand. "Actually, Uncle Jake, I don't understand. I'm a kid. I don't have a job. How can I earn it?"

"Two ways. First, you are going to fix up this bike. Not

only are you going to get it working again, you are going to make it *nice* so you can sell it to earn some
money. And second, you are going to get a job. There is
no reason a healthy kid like you can't find a way to
make money."

"Doing what?" I asked, not sure if this was the most
realistic plan in the world. I was a kid, for crying out
loud!

"Doing work," Uncle Jake replied. "Now, let's go get
cleaned up."

And with that, we walked out of the garage and
back to the house. It seemed like my whole summer just
changed.

CHAPTER 6: TROUBLE AGAIN

Today was the first day of camp at the rec center and it was AWFUL!

First of all, I had to leave my house at 7:30 a.m. to walk there. Since I had to leave at 7:30 a.m., it meant I had to get up EVEN EARLIER than normal to work out. I asked Uncle Jake if I could skip the morning workout because I had to go to camp. You know what he said? "No." That's it! "No." So I woke up early and worked out with Uncle Jake—and I have to admit, I felt better when I was done, like I always do.

Then I had to walk to the rec center. And, yes, I said WALK because, if you remember, I DON'T HAVE A BIKE! I was pretty much the ONLY KID WALKING. Almost every

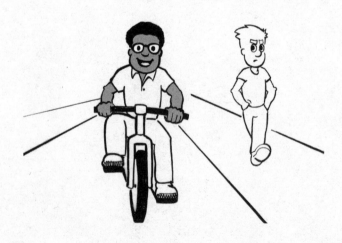

other kid rode a bike. There were even two kids with the Bentlee bike! And I had NOTHING!

So I was already not in a good mood when I got there. Then who is the first person that actually talks to me at the camp? Nathan James! And you know what he says? He says, "How was the last day of school, trouble-maker?" Nathan James! Calling ME a troublemaker! I WAS MAD.

But I remembered Uncle Jake telling me that warriors don't lose control of their emotions and that they definitely don't lose their tempers.

So I tried to calm myself down. "The last day of school was okay," I told Nathan plainly, hoping he would just leave me alone.

"I had fun," he said with a big smile on his face,

knowing that I DID NOT HAVE FUN on the last day of school.

I didn't even answer. But I started getting mad. REALLY MAD. I was thinking that if he said ONE MORE THING TO ME, I was going to go CRAZY. I could feel my face turning redder and redder and my hands starting to clench into fists.

Then suddenly a voice said, "Good morning, kids. Come on over here and let's get you signed in." It was one of the camp counselors getting all the kids to come sign in for the day.

Nathan said, "Sure," smiled his annoying little smile at me, and walked away. I was fuming! I could barely even move.

A different counselor looked at me and said, "Are you okay, kid? Go over there and sign in."

I wasn't okay. I was mad. But I walked over to the sign-in desk and put my signature next to my name.

MARC
Print Name

Signature

I could barely even write, I was so mad!

For the rest of the day, we did a bunch of activities. We did some art, which I am pretty good at, so that was okay. Then we played baseball, which I am NOT GOOD AT, and it was not fun.

Every time I got up to bat, I could feel Nathan looking at me, staring at me with his stupid smile. I hated it! And it kept getting worse, because I struck out EVERY TIME. And every time I swung and missed, I could hear Nathan say, "Good one, champ!" or "Nice swing, champ," or "A swing and a miss!" He was talking just loud enough that I could hear him but quiet enough that the counselors could not hear him.

AAAHHHHHHHHHH! It was driving me crazy. And the madder I got, THE WORSE I DID.

Then, after the millionth time I swung and missed, I heard Nathan say, "Another good one, champ!" from way in the outfield.

That was it. I yelled at the top of my lungs:

"SHUT UP, NATHAN, YOU IDIOT!"

Now this might not have been too big of a deal, but it was one of those moments where everything got quiet just as I started to yell, so everyone heard exactly what I said. On top of that, because I was so mad, it was the LOUDEST YELL EVER, and since I was so mad, everyone could tell I was mad!

"Hey!" one of the counselors shouted. "Get over here." I walked over to the counselor, who was sitting on the side of the field. "Come with me." He walked me away from the field and brought me to the rec center office. "I don't know what your problem is, but you can't act like that here."

"I'm sorry," I told him, and I was, too. I knew I shouldn't have acted that way. "But that kid was calling me names and making fun of me all morning."

"I don't care what he was calling you," the counselor said, "and you shouldn't care what someone calls you, either. If you have another outburst like that again, I'm going to have to call your parents. You understand me?"

"Yes. I do."

AAAAHHHHHHHHHH!!! This was the second time in a week that I had been in trouble because of NATHAN JAMES. I couldn't stand him.

Then, as I sat there and thought about it, I had an idea. An idea that would solve this problem once and for all: I would fight him. I knew jiu-jitsu, and I knew I could beat him in a fight. So I would fight him and shut him up once and for all! I suddenly started to feel better.

You see, I figured out right then and there that Nathan was pretty much like Kenny Williamson last year in school, but instead of bullying people by pushing them around, Nathan is a bully with his words. But his words seem to hurt just as bad as getting punched in the face!

When I stood up to Kenny Williamson, he realized that he shouldn't act the way he was acting. If I fought Nathan, he would learn the same lesson: that if you treat people badly, there are consequences.

I would teach Nathan that lesson.

CHAPTER 7: RED FLARES

When I got home, I decided I would tell Uncle Jake about everything that happened today. I figured he would be proud that I had decided to fight Nathan. Boy, was I wrong.

"How did it go at camp today?" Uncle Jake asked me.

"Not good," I replied.

"Not good? Why not?" he asked.

I explained everything that happened. What Nathan said when I first saw him. How horrible baseball was, but how it was even worse because of Nathan making fun of me. How mad I got. What I yelled and how I yelled it, and how I got in trouble with the counselor.

And, you know, I thought that Uncle Jake might have thought this was kind of cool. At least a little bit. At least the part when I yelled back at Nathan and called him an idiot.

I also thought there was a chance that Uncle Jake might be mad at me for getting in trouble. After all, he had already picked me up from the office at school and wasn't happy about me getting in trouble then, so I thought this might make him REALLY mad.

But when I finished telling him the whole story, I

couldn't tell if he thought it was cool or if he was mad at me. He just sat there quietly for a few seconds. Then he finally said, "I guess you didn't understand what I told you the other day about controlling your emotions, did you?"

"What?" I asked him, since I didn't remember at all what he was talking about.

"Your emotions. The other day when I picked you up from school and you were angry and frustrated and crying, I explained to you that those were emotions you need to control, because when people don't control their emotions, they make bad decisions. Do you remember that?"

"Yes, Uncle Jake. I remember."

Emotional me
is no way to be.

"Then why did you act emotional again today? Why did you get in trouble? Why did you give Nathan the satisfaction of knowing that he got into your head and made you lose control?"

Sheesh! With all those questions, Uncle Jake just made me feel like I was a big baby. But it wasn't as easy as he made it sound.

"But Nathan is SO ANNOYING! He gets under my skin with the little things he says, and the way he acts makes me so mad. And today I stayed calm at first, but he just kept talking and talking and making fun of me and I just . . . I just . . ."

"You lost control." Uncle Jake finished my sentence. "You lost control of your emotions."

"Yes. Yes, I did, Uncle Jake."

"And look at what happened and what you did when you lost control of your emotions. You performed worse at baseball. You let Nathan know how much he was bothering you. And you got in trouble. All those out-comes are bad. On top of those, Nathan probably feels like he won. He was trying to annoy you—and he suc-

Guess who's
number one, baby?

52

ceeded. When you yelled back at him and got in trouble, he was laughing. He had accomplished his mission. By getting emotional, you let him win."

I understood what Uncle Jake was trying to say, but I still didn't understand how to actually control my emotions, like he was saying. "I get it, Uncle Jake. But it's not that easy. When he says all those things, it isn't like I choose to get mad at him. I can't stop it. I can't control it. It just happens. How am I supposed to stop it?"

"Good question, Marc," Uncle Jake said. "Let me ask you this: When you start to get mad, what do you notice about yourself?"

"What do I notice? I don't really notice anything—I'm too busy being mad!" I told him.

"No. I'm not talking about when you are mad. I'm talking about *before* you're mad. When you are starting to get mad. What do you notice then?"

"Well. I start to feel kind of hot."

"Okay. That's what a lot of people feel when they are getting mad. What else?"

"I feel like my face is turning red."

"Okay. That's very common. What else?"

"When I'm really starting to get mad, I squeeze my hands into fists, like I am ready to fight!"

"Yep," Uncle Jake said. "Those are all normal responses and what people feel when they are starting to get mad. Those are red flares that tell you there is an emergency—that you are losing control of your emotions."

"*Red flares?* What is a *red flare?*"

"A red flare is a universal signal for an emergency. If you are in a boat that is sinking, you can send up a red flare and people will know you need help. If you are lost in the woods, you can set off a red flare. Even in the SEAL Teams, when we were on an operation and there was a problem and we couldn't get help through our radios, we would fire off a red flare as an alert that we needed help. So a red flare is a signal that help is needed. When you start feeling hot or feeling your face turn red or you feel yourself clenching your fists, then that is a signal to yourself that you need help. You need to get control of your emotions."

"Are all emotions bad?"

"No! Not at all. Emotions are good. They make you who you are. They allow you to feel. Happiness and gratitude are good. Joy and excitement are good. Love is a good emotion. So is satisfaction—when you feel like you have accomplished something. Those are all good emotions, but even good emotions need to be controlled. You already know it isn't smart to celebrate with joy before you actually accomplish a goal. Even emotions you might think are bad aren't bad—emotions like anger, fear, and frustration. They also make you who you are. But you have to learn how to make sure those emotions don't get out of control. Because, as a warrior, those emotions can cause you to make mistakes or bad decisions, and in war, bad decisions can cost lives. So warriors have to keep their emotions under control."

"Well, I learned how to deal with my fear last summer when I jumped off Bird Bridge," I told Uncle Jake.

"You certainly did. So you know you can do it. You can control your emotions. And in order to do that, the first thing you have to be able to do is recognize what your red flares are."

"What do red flares have to do with emotions?" I asked Uncle Jake.

"I'm not talking about actual red flares. Like I said, a red flare is used in many places as a warning—a warning against some kind of danger. But in this case, red flares are signals that show you are in danger of losing your temper."

"Signals? What kinds of signals could tell me that?" I asked.

"The signals you just told me about. Feeling hot. Turning red. Feeling your hands squeezing into fists. Those are

I have to learn to cool down.

all signals telling you that you are about to lose your temper—and once that happens, you can get your emotions under control."

"How do I do that? Just because I know the emotions are coming doesn't mean I can stop them!" I told Uncle Jake.

"No. I didn't say you could stop them. But you can definitely get them under control."

"Okay. Then how do I get them under control?"

"There are a bunch of things you can do. First of all, remember that losing control of your emotions is what babies do and that warriors keep themselves calm. You have to detach from those emotions—step back from them a little so they don't control you. You can do that by taking a deep breath and telling yourself to calm down. Or try thinking about something else, something that doesn't make you feel frustrated. If none of that works and you simply cannot calm yourself down, then just walk away. You don't have to be rude or anything

when you do that, either. You just say 'Excuse me,' and walk away. Get yourself away from the situation that is making you lose control. That will hopefully calm you down by actually detaching you from what is happening. And even if it doesn't calm you down, at least you got away from the place where losing your temper might get you into some kind of trouble. Does this make sense to you?" Uncle Jake asked.

It actually did. "Yes, Uncle Jake. It makes sense. Warrior Kids should not be losing their tempers. So I need to look for 'red flares,' which are warning signs that tell me I'm losing my temper, like getting hot or turning red. I get it. And I will definitely try to watch for the red flares. Because my emotions seem to keep getting me into trouble."

"Yes, they do, Marc. Yes, they do," Uncle Jake said. "And it is time to get them under control."

"I will, Uncle Jake. I will."

CHAPTER 8: BUSINESS OWNER

So today was Saturday. What does a normal kid do on Saturday? Maybe sleep in, relax, watch some TV?

Nope. Not for me. Today was hard work, but it was also AWESOME.

First, Uncle Jake and I got up and did a really cool workout. We did ten pull-ups, then a sprint to the end of the driveway and back, and then twenty push-ups and another sprint to the end of the driveway and back. We did that ten times. And even though Uncle Jake did it faster than me, I still DID IT!

When we got done with the workout, Uncle Jake had me bring my old, rusty bike into the garage. Then we got out my dad's tools, and Uncle Jake told me, "Okay. Now take it apart."

"Take what apart?" I asked him.

"The bicycle," he told me.

"What part of it should I take apart?" I asked.

"All of it," Uncle Jake said.

"All of it?"

"Yes. All of it. This whole bike needs to be cleaned up and have the rust removed, and some parts need to get oiled up. So, yes. All of it."

"Okay," I told Uncle Jake as he handed me a wrench and pointed to the front tire. I took the wrench from him and began to take off the front tire. It was pretty rusted up, but I cranked hard on the wrench and eventually it came loose on one side. But the other side wouldn't budge.

"That's what happens when you don't take care of things," Uncle Jake said as he handed me a spray bottle.

"Spray some of that on there and let it soak for a few minutes," he continued. I followed his instructions, sprayed it on, and let it sit for a few minutes. Then I tried again, and it came off.

"Get the pedals off next," he said.

So I took off the pedals, then the seat and the chain guard before taking off the back tire and the chain and finally the brakes. As I took off each piece, Uncle Jake had me put it on the floor in a very specific place—basically putting each part of the bike on the ground close to where it would be if the bike were assembled but lying on its side. When I finally set the brake parts down on the ground, I was done.

"Okay. Now what?" I asked Uncle Jake.

"Now you have to remove all the rust from all of these parts and prime them for paint," he said.

"Okay . . . but how?" I asked.

"Well, there is your first problem. You see, your dad doesn't have all the right tools for this job. You need a wire brush and some metal sandpaper. And when you are done removing the rust, you will need some primer paint and some colored paint for the paint job. You are going to need to buy those."

"But I don't have any money," I said sadly.

"You will."

Yes, I thought to myself. *Uncle Jake is going to give me money!*

"Thanks so much, Uncle Jake! Thanks for giving me some money to get this bike fixed up! You're the best uncle ever."

Uncle Jake laughed. "Give you money?! Ha! That isn't happening. If I gave you money, I wouldn't be the best uncle—not at all."

Umm . . . we don't hang out with lazy people.

"Ummm, actually, Uncle Jake, I think you would be AWESOME if you gave me the money I need to get this bike all fixed up!"

Uncle Jake shook his head. "That's what a lot of people would think. But they would be wrong. It's like I told you the other day: If I just give you the money, then you wouldn't have earned it. It wouldn't mean anything to you. You wouldn't understand the hard work and time it takes to earn that money. Then you won't appreciate what you do with the money, and you won't think you need to take care of the things you buy with your money.

That's why you are going to get a job."

"Uncle Jake, it actually does sound pretty cool to earn my own money. But there is one major problem here."

"What's that?"

"Well, Uncle Jake, it is the same problem I told you about the last time we talked about this: If you haven't noticed, I'm a KID! I'm only eleven years old! How can I get a job? Jobs are for adults! What business would hire a kid?"

"Well then, Marc, I guess you are going to have to create your own business."

Now this made absolutely no sense to me AT ALL. What was he talking about? Had my uncle Jake gone crazy? "Uncle Jake, let me say this again. I'm only ELEVEN YEARS OLD! How can I start a business?"

"It is actually pretty simple," Uncle Jake replied. "Think of something that you can do that other people don't like doing."

"What?" I asked Uncle Jake. I didn't understand where he was going with this.

"What can you do that other people don't want to do? What skills do you have?"

"Uncle Jake, I know I am a Warrior Kid and I can work out and do jiu-jitsu. But THAT DOESN'T CHANGE THE FACT THAT I'M ELEVEN YEARS OLD! What skill do I possibly have that I could turn into a business?!?!"

Uncle Jake stared at me for a few seconds. Then he said, "Come with me." He walked out of the garage. I followed him as he walked across the yard to the shed that my bike had been leaning against. He opened the door and said, "There you go."

I had no idea what he was talking about.

"I don't get it. What?"

He pointed to the back corner of the shed, at my dad's lawn mower. "You are going to mow lawns. That is something that most people really don't feel like doing—and it is something that you can do. Add those two things together and you have yourself a business."

Uncle Jake was right again! No, mowing lawns isn't fun—which is why most people don't like doing it (including my mom and dad!). But I can do it, and I already do it for my parents, so why not do it for other people as well and get paid for it?

"YES! That's a great idea, Uncle Jake! I can do that. And I'm pretty good at it, too! I am a business owner! ME!"

MY 1ˢᵗ BUSINESS PARTNER!

"Hold on there, Marc," Uncle Jake said.

I got worried that there was something I hadn't thought of. Some problem. "What is it, Uncle Jake?"

"Well, if you own a business, then your business needs a name. What is your business going to be called?"

I thought for a minute. Then the answer jumped into my head. "Marc's Meticulous Mowing!" I shouted out.

"I like it!" Uncle Jake said. "Congratulations, business owner."

"Thanks, Uncle Jake!" I shouted.

And that was it. Today I became Marc: Warrior Kid and Business Owner. YES! AWESOME!

CHAPTER 9: THE LAST RESORT

I was a warrior today. I kept my cool and controlled my emotions. But I'm not sure it is going to help, because there is still a major problem.

That problem is Nathan.

It started when I got to camp today. Of course Nathan was there, and of course Nathan was being his normal self—MEAN. I don't know what his problem is! We were all hanging around and getting ready to play kickball. I was talking to Jessica. She is one of those people who is really good at every sport there is. Soccer, baseball, kickball, basketball—anything and everything. I was asking her what her favorite sport was since she is so good at all of them.

"Probably basketball," she told me. "I like it because it is fast and you get to score a lot! What is your favorite sport?"

"That's cool," I told her. "I like basketball, too."

"Is it your favorite?" she asked.

At this point I realized that Nathan was there and that he was listening to Jessica and I talk. I just knew he was going to say something! But I just ignored him and started to answer her question. "My favor–" Just as I started talking, Nathan cut me off.

"Yeah . . . what's your favorite sport, PLATE FACE?" he said in a weird, high-pitched voice, mocking Jessica.

I stood there for a second. I tried to ignore him and started again. "My favorite spor–"

"Hello. My name is Plate Face. What's my favorite sport?" Nathan interrupted, this time in another strange voice that was supposed to be me.

That was it. I started to get mad. Really mad. The feeling flooded over me like a tidal wave! I felt my face getting hotter and knew it was starting to turn red. Then

my fists started to get tighter. All these things were exactly what Uncle Jake had called red flares. I was losing control of my emotions! I was about to lose my temper. I knew this was not good. So I did what Uncle Jake told me to do. I stepped outside the situation in my head and took a deep breath. I told myself to calm down, because Warrior Kids don't lose control of their emotions. This was how I got in trouble at school, and I wasn't going to let that happen again. I felt better already. Now I needed a way to get out of the situation—to get away from Nathan.

So instead of responding to Nathan, I looked at Jessica and said, "Do you want to go to the water fountain before the game?"

"Okay," she said, looking very relieved that we would be able to get away from Nathan. We walked away,

toward the water fountain. As we walked, I could hear Nathan continuing to talk loudly about something, but I just ignored him.

Jessica and I went and got a drink.

"That kid Nathan is mean," Jessica told me after she got a drink.

"Yeah, he is," I answered. "But I think the best thing to do is just ignore him."

"That's true. But it can be kind of hard to ignore him since he is so LOUD!" she said, raising her voice LOUDLY at the end of her sentence and making a funny face. We laughed and then walked back over toward the group by the kickball field. As we got closer, the first thing I heard was Nathan. He was talking to this other kid, Bobby.

"How do you even fit a brain inside your tiny skull? Your head is so little. Mosquito head . . . that's what you are. Mosquito Head!"

Bobby didn't look happy at all. He was a shy kid, and now Nathan was making him the center of attention—and not for a good reason!

"Please don't suck out my blood, Mosquito Head!"

Bobby mumbled, "I'm not going to do that. I'm not a Mosqu—"

"LOOK! Mosquito Head can actually talk! Not very

loudly, because of his tiny little mouth on his tiny little head, but he can talk!!!"

I could see the look on Bobby's face. He didn't know what to do or say. He looked like he was about to cry. It made me MAD—even madder than when Nathan was making fun of me. I started to feel my anger come up again—and once again, I got control of my emotions. I took another deep breath to calm down.

But I wasn't the only one who thought Bobby was about to cry. "Oh, look! Mosquito Head is about to cry some mosquito tears!" Nathan shouted.

Even though I had my emotions under control, I still remembered my Warrior Kid Code. It said that a Warrior Kid stands up to bullies and helps out other people whenever possible. Well, Bobby needed my help. I needed to shut Nathan up RIGHT NOW. It was time for my jiu-jitsu to get used. I pushed through the crowd and walked right up to Nathan.

"That's enough, Nathan. Be quiet. No one wants to hear you," I told him in a calm but serious voice.

"Who asked you?" Nathan shouted back. "And what are you going to do about it?"

"Well," I said, "if you keep talking, you will find out."

Nathan started to say something back when he got cut off. "All right, kids! Let's line up to pick teams." It was one of the camp counselors who had just come out to the field. He had no idea what had just happened—or what was about to happen—when he walked up.

We all lined up, and a couple of kids got picked to be team captains and pick the rest of the teams. But I wasn't paying attention to that. I was thinking about fighting Nathan. As a Warrior Kid, I am supposed to help other people. Kids like Bobby needed my help. I needed to stand up for them.

When I got home at the end of the day, I told Uncle Jake the whole story. I explained how I detached and controlled my emotions and walked away from Nathan. Then I told him about what Nathan had said to Bobby and that he actually did this to all kinds of kids. I explained to him that Nathan is just a mean person and won't ever change. Finally I said, "I am going to fight Nathan."

Uncle Jake sat there for a little while, quietly. Then he said, "Are you sure about that?"

"Yes," I told him, "I'm sure. He has a horrible attitude. No matter what anyone says to him, he never stops. I need to stop him."

Uncle Jake was quiet again and finally said, "Okay, Marc. If that is what needs to happen, then that is what needs to happen. But fighting should always be a last resort. You should not fight unless you absolutely have to—unless there are no other options at all. And even then, before you fight, you have to make sure you're doing the right thing and you have to find out more about the person you are going to fight. In the SEAL Teams, we call it *gathering intelligence*."

"'Gathering intelligence'? What's that?" I asked.

"Finding out about the person you are going to fight. What are they capable of? What sort of weapons do they have? What is driving them? Do they have any people who might come to help them—people you would have to watch out for? And figure out why they are acting the way they are acting. There is always a chance that if we know why someone is acting a certain way, maybe we can attack that reason instead of attacking them."

"Okay. But what intelligence should I gather about Nathan? I already know what I need to know! He is a loudmouth and a bully!"

"There is a lot more you need to know. You need to try and find out what makes him like this. Find out everything you can. What kind of shoes he has. What kind of backpack he carries. What he brings to camp for snacks.

Who he hangs around with. Everything. That way you know exactly who you are dealing with if it gets to the point that you have to fight."

"So is it kind of like spying on him?"

"No. Just observing him. Watching. Listening. Learning about him. Take notes so you can explain everything to me. Does that make sense?"

"Yes, Uncle Jake. I got it."

"Okay. Great. Now make it happen."

And that was it. When I thought about it more, I realized that Uncle Jake had just given me my first mission! "Gather intelligence." It even sounded cool! And I also realized that Uncle Jake had just given me permission to fight Nathan when my mission was completed. Finally, I would be able to use my jiu-jitsu for real and become a true Warrior Kid.

CHAPTER 10: UNCOMFORTABLE

Today was a pretty good day. UNTIL I GOT HOME FROM JIU-JITSU.

My morning workout was good. I actually set a new personal record in pull-ups! I did twenty-two in one set. That's a heck of a lot better than what I could do last year: ZERO! Even Uncle Jake was pretty impressed with twenty-two. So that was a great way to start off the day.

ALWAYS PULL-UP!

From there, I had breakfast and then walked to camp. Okay, walking was not good—I should have a bike! But I got there, and when I did, everything was good at camp, too. We split into groups for activities, and Nathan wasn't in my group, so it was actually pretty fun. We did a cool art project and then we played games with eggs, trying not to break them as we played catch and carried them in spoons and passed them down a big line using only our elbows.

The last thing we did with the eggs was build contraptions with straws and tape and cardboard that protected the eggs when we dropped them off a twelve-foot ladder. My team's egg survived the drop in the contraption we built!

When I got home, I worked on the bike for a while and then went to jiu-jitsu class. Jiu-jitsu class was fun. We learned two awesome moves and then we rolled a bunch. Rolling jiu-jitsu is REALLY fun—it is basically when you fight against the other person, only you don't actually fight. You don't punch or kick each other. And of course you don't scratch or bite each other, either! But it feels like a fight. What you are doing is grappling against each other, trying to grip and pull and move your opponent into a position where you can control them.

Once you have control over them, you try to use a submission hold on them to make them *tap out*, which means they give up. The submission hold might be on their elbow or their shoulder, or it might be a choke—but once you have it, they know you have it and they tap out to give up.

Of course, it isn't always me that gets the submission hold. Sometimes I get beat, too, and that is okay. Because every time you tap out, you actually learn from it. You learn what mistake you made to end up there. And you learn what you can do to avoid it happening again. So tapping out—even though you are losing—isn't that big of a deal in practice.

At the end of class, I noticed that Uncle Jake was there and that he was watching me. He had a big smile on his face, and I could tell that he was happy to see me train and actually know what I was doing. He also saw me tap out a few kids, which was cool.

When class was over, Uncle Jake and I went out to the car. As soon as we got inside the car, he said, "How do you like jiu-jitsu?" with a big smile on his face. I think he already knew the answer.

"It's awesome," I told him. "It is super fun."

"What do you like about it?"

"I don't know exactly. Pretty much everything. I guess

the main thing is that I like how all the moves fit together and one move leads to another move, which leads to another move, which leads to another move. And when you put the moves together, it's like a special power!"

"I know! It's awesome, isn't it?" Uncle Jake asked me enthusiastically.

"Yeah!" I told him.

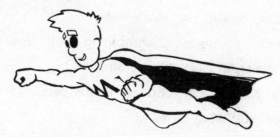

Then his whole face and attitude changed in a millisecond.

"Then why aren't you going to compete?"

His change in attitude confused me for a second.

"What?" I asked him.

"Why don't you compete? You told me your instructor wants you to compete but you're not doing it. Why not? You are good. You need to test yourself."

I should have known this was coming! Just when my day was going perfect! I didn't know what to say. So I just sat there.

After a minute or so, Uncle Jake said, "Well?"

"'Well' what?" I responded, hoping somehow that he

had forgotten what we were talking about. Then he said it slowly and clearly.

"Why . . . don't . . . you . . . compete?"

I sat and thought about the answer. But I didn't want to tell him. So I started to make something up. "Because . . . I'm . . . it's just not my style."

"Not your style? You are good at it! It is definitely your style! That doesn't make any sense."

"Well . . . I mean . . . competing . . . competing isn't really my style. I just like to train."

"But your coach wants you to compete."

"But I just want to train."

Uncle Jake was quiet for a minute. Then he said, "Why do you want to train?"

"What?"

"Training? Why do you like to train?"

"Because it's fun. And I want to get better."

"Okay. That makes sense. Then why don't you want to compete? It's still jiu-jitsu. And competition makes you better."

"I know . . . but . . . I just–"

"Wait," Uncle Jake cut me off. "Are you scared?"

I knew I just had to come clean. So I told him, "Yeah. Yeah, I am. I'm scared."

"Scared of what? Sheesh! You are really good. You do

jiu-jitsu all the time! How can you possibly be scared of something that you do every day?"

"It's not jiu-jitsu that I'm scared of!" I told him, and I kind of even raised my voice—getting a little emotional. Uncle Jake seemed to sense that and stayed quiet for a little bit, which calmed me down.

"Okay, then. What are you scared of?" he asked me calmly.

I thought about how to tell him for a minute, and finally, I just said it: "Losing. I don't want to lose."

Uncle Jake nodded his head. "Good," he said.

"Good?" I asked. "How is that good?"

"I want you to be scared of losing. I want you to be really scared of losing. Why? Because fear will make you train harder. Fear will make you work harder. Fear will make you prepare more. And when you do all those things, your chances of success go up."

"But I can still lose," I told him.

"Not really. You only really lose if you don't try, if you let your fear keep you from even getting in the game or on the mat. That is how you lose. But if you get out there and do your best, you will either win, or you will learn. Either way, it is good for you."

"But what if I do horrible? What if I get tapped out in ten seconds?! Then what?"

"'Then what?' Like I said, if that is the case, then you learn. You learn what mistake you made. You learn what part of your game you need to work on. You learn what moves you need to practice. Warriors don't always just do what they want to do. They don't stay in a nice, comfortable world. They push themselves to be uncomfortable. That is how warriors make themselves better. You should do the same thing. Push yourself to do things you

I'm not going to be easy on you . . . I mean me . . . I mean . . .

don't want to do. Does that make sense?"

It did make sense, but I still wasn't quite sure about it. "I guess so," I told him.

"Okay. Well, think about it. It will make you better."

I was thinking about it. Like always, Uncle Jake made sense. And even though I wasn't quite ready to say yes just yet, I knew it was the right thing to do and I had to do it.

CHAPTER 11: THE FEELING OF FREEDOM

I thought I understood what Discipline Equals Freedom meant when Uncle Jake taught me about it last summer. It means that, in order to have freedom in life, you have to have discipline, you have to work hard, and you have to do some things that you might not want to do. And I worked hard, studying and training and exercising in order to be free from bullies and from feeling dumb in class and from feeling weak. But I've been learning A LOT more about the discipline of hard work this summer!

Last weekend Uncle Jake had me make up flyers for my Meticulous Mowing service and hand them out around the neighborhood. He also had me add another "service" to the flyer: PULLING WEEDS. Now, if you've ever pulled weeds before, you know how hard it is. You are

on your hands and knees, digging into the roots of weeds and pulling them out, and when a yard hasn't been taken care of, there can be MILLIONS of weeds. I told Uncle Jake I didn't want to pull weeds. He told me, "I know that. Neither does anyone else! That's why you will get good money to do it!" Once again, what Uncle Jake was saying made sense. Of course no one likes pulling weeds—that's why they would pay me to do it.

Well, during the week, six people called my house and asked for either their lawn to be mowed or weeds to be pulled or both! When I got the messages, Uncle Jake had me call them back each day when I got home from camp and set a time during the weekend when I could come by and do the work. By the time Friday came around, I had both Saturday and Sunday filled with appointments! I figured it would take me about one hour per house, but Uncle Jake told me to schedule enough time for it to take two hours per house, so that's what I did.

I figured that, since I was going to be working most of the day, maybe on Saturday I would sleep in. I didn't set my alarm. I FIGURED WRONG!

I was lying there, dreaming about a nice, cold mint-chocolate-chip milkshake, when suddenly my covers were ripped off me and Uncle Jake was standing above me. "Good morning, sunshine. What are you do-ing? Why aren't you down in the garage for our workout?"

"Well, I'm going to be working almost the whole day today, so I figured I could relax a little bit this morning."

"Sure. You could. If you don't mind being weak! Just because you have other things to do doesn't mean you should skip workouts. In fact, if you go through life only working out when things are perfect and you have plenty of time, then you won't work out very much at all. Even in the SEAL Teams, sometimes we get really busy with training or operations. The good SEALs would still work out to make sure they're staying in shape. When you miss workouts, you can't make them up. They are gone. So why don't you get up, get down to the garage, and get after it?"

"Okay, Uncle Jake, I'll be down in a minute," I told

him. So I got up, put my workout clothes on, and headed down to the garage. Once I was down there and started exercising, I felt better and was glad I did.

Afterward, it was time for me to go do my work on the lawns. First it was the O'Tooles' house. Theirs was pretty easy because the yard was small. Then it was the Kirths' house, which took longer because I had to move a bunch of lawn furniture before I started mowing the lawn and then put it all back when I was done. The last house of the day was the Wiltberrys', and that one took forever. First of all, it was a big lawn. Second, they had stuff all over it that I had to move. And third, they had all kinds of weeds for me to pull. There were weeds around the driveway, around their little sidewalk, and even around a little garden they had. It took forever! I didn't get back to my house until three thirty in the

afternoon. And when I got back, I was tired and dirty and hungry and thirsty, and I felt like it had been a very, very long day. But guess what?

I HAD TWENTY-ONE DOLLARS!!!!!!!!!!!!!

TWENTY-ONE DOLLARS—ALL MINE!!! FROM JUST ONE DAY OF WORK!!!

As soon as I got home, I showed Uncle Jake. He was excited, too! "Nice work, Marc. Or should I say *magnificent?*"

"Say whatever you want! I'm happy, and I'm also tired. I'm going to go sit down and relax for a bit," I told Uncle Jake.

"What?" Uncle Jake said in a tone that made me nervous—like he had more for me to do.

"I said I'm going to go sit down for a bit and relax. I'm really tired."

"Aren't you forgetting something?"

I didn't know what Uncle Jake was talking about. "Not that I can think of," I told him.

"What about your bike?" he said.

Oh no. I *had* forgotten something. I was supposed to work on my bike for at least thirty minutes every day—no matter what. But I thought today must be different since I had already worked for almost six hours—plus my morning workout. It had been a LONG DAY. So I figured I would just explain to Uncle Jake that I was tired and he would understand. "Well, since I have been working all day, I figured maybe I could take a break from working on the bike."

I SHOULD HAVE KNOWN BETTER!

"That's not how things work. That's not what warriors do. When warriors commit to a job, they do it. What you are doing is called *procrastination*. Putting things off. Saying that you will do things later. That doesn't work. When a warrior has something to do, they do it and do it right away."

"But . . ." I started to explain to Uncle Jake that maybe today I could just use a little break. But he wasn't being a very good listener.

Sorry, I can't
hear excuses
very well . . .

"Don't 'but' me. There are no buts. If you don't complete the work, then the work doesn't get done. And once you do it and it is done, you won't have to worry about it anymore. I promise that once you do the work, you WILL be glad you did. Now. Quit debating this with me, and go out and get to work."

Well, when Uncle Jake says "no debating," that pretty much means no debating. So I walked straight out to the garage and got to work on the bike. I focused on cleaning the rust off of the front rim. I had a little scouring pad meant for metal surfaces and the rust-busting spray that Uncle Jake had given me for the rusty bolts. I scrubbed it pretty hard, and as I did, the rust came off. After the rim itself looked pretty good, I cleaned each individual spoke. It took a little longer than I thought, especially the areas where the spokes went into the rim—it was small and hard to get the scouring pad into those tight areas. But eventually I did it, and when it was all done, the front rim looked GREAT.

Sunday was almost a repeat of Saturday—except I didn't even try to get out of the morning workout or working on the bike. I just did what I knew I needed to do. I got up early, worked out, loaded my Meticulous Mowing gear into a bucket, pushed the mower to the houses of the Kellys, the Butlers, and the Wards, mowed their lawns, pulled their weeds, walked back to my house, went straight to the garage, and started to clean and scour the bike's back rim.

When I was about done, Uncle Jake came in.

"Look at the rims, Uncle Jake," I said as I held up one rim and pointed to the other. "They look awesome!"

"They sure do, Marc. That's great. And how much money did you make today?"

"Another twenty-one dollars!" I said. "That's a total of forty-two! In one weekend!"

"How does it all feel?" Uncle Jake asked.

That's kind of a silly question, I thought to myself. *It feels AWESOME, of course.*

"AWESOME. It feels awesome!"

"Are you sure?"

"Am I sure? Of course I am! I have forty-two dollars and my bike rims look practically brand-new!"

Uncle Jake stood with a big smile on his face for a minute. Then he said, "I want you to remember this feeling. It's a great feeling, the feeling of having worked hard and gotten something done. But sometimes we forget how good it feels. So we don't do what we should. This is the same as how Discipline Equals Freedom. The discipline is the hard work. The freedom is the freedom to buy what you want because you have worked for the money. It is the freedom to ride a bike instead of walking. The freedom is also that feeling, that good feeling of accomplishment. It's freedom from feeling that you wasted time. Does that make sense?"

"It does, Uncle Jake. Just like the discipline of studying and working out and training jiu-jitsu gave me freedom, the discipline of working hard for what I want also gives me freedom. And, of course, the freedom feels good."

"That's the feeling I want you to remember—the feeling of freedom and accomplishment—especially when you have hard work ahead of you. Will you remember that feeling?"

"Yes, Uncle Jake. I will," I told him. And I meant it.

CHAPTER 12: OLD SHOES

For the past few days I have been gathering intelligence on Nathan. I learned a lot. I did this by using *surveillance*, which is another cool thing I learned from Uncle Jake. It means to watch something very closely and take note so that you really understand someone, what they do, and why they do it. Uncle Jake gave me some instructions on how to gather intelligence by using surveillance.

He told me to get close but not too close. To stay at a distance and watch but to make sure that I was actually doing something and not just standing there watching. So I figured out some good ways to make that happen. When Nathan was playing baseball, I watched him from the jungle gym while doing some sets of pull-ups and other easy exercises. During lunch, I sat two tables away, facing him so I could see him but still not stare at him. I would just eat my lunch and watch him out of my *peripheral vision*. Uncle Jake taught me about peripheral vision. It means that you aren't staring right at something but you are instead watching it from the sides of your vision. COOL! Also, when we were in the classroom for art or in the library for reading, I would sit a couple of tables away. Again, I would do whatever project or assignment we were supposed to, but I would make sure that I was sitting in such a way that I could see what Nathan was doing.

The first day I completely FAILED! When I got home, Uncle Jake asked me to write down everything I learned about Nathan. So I did. I only wrote *He talks a lot* and gave it to Uncle Jake.

"That's it?" Uncle Jake asked me.

"Well. Yeah. I guess. That's what I saw."

"We already knew he talked a lot! Mission failure!" Uncle Jake said with a smile on his face.

"Mission failure? No way! I watched him all day!"

"You watched him, but you didn't see anything," Uncle Jake said.

"Okay. Now I'm confused. What the heck does that mean?"

Uncle Jake looked at me for a few seconds, then said, "It means that you didn't actually gather any intelligence. We are trying to find out everything we can about Nathan. All you figured out is what we already know. You need to look for details. How does he get to school? What kind of shoes does he wear? What kind of socks? What does he eat for lunch? What kind of backpack does he have, and what does he keep in there? How does he get home from school? Find out everything you can."

I didn't understand why this was important at all. Who cared about all this stuff? "Why is all this stuff important, Uncle Jake? I already know he is a mean kid. I should just fight him and get it over with!"

Uncle Jake shook his head and then said sharply, "No, Marc. NO. That is not what we do. We don't go around fighting people just because they are annoying. That is an emotional move, and remember: Warriors don't act on emotions. Warriors have to understand *why* they are fighting. Right now, you don't know. But if you can figure that out, then we can make a logical decision about how to solve this problem. That might mean a fight, but it should really mean something else. Fighting is only a last resort, if all your other solutions have failed. As warriors, we are prepared to fight, but we avoid it if we can."

"Okay, Uncle Jake. I get that part, but I sure don't

understand what his lunch and shoes and backpack have to do with any of this," I told him.

"We need to understand our problem. If we don't fully understand a problem, then we can't solve it in the most efficient way possible. So stop complaining and gather better intelligence tomorrow at school."

"Okay, Uncle Jake. I will."

So the next few days I did what Uncle Jake said. Here are some things I figured out about Nathan:

1. Nathan has old shoes. In fact, his shoes are so old that there are holes in the soles, and his right shoe actually has a hole in the bottom that goes all the way through to his sock.

2. Speaking of socks, his are dirty and don't match. They also look like maybe a dog chewed on them.

3. Nathan's pants have holes in one knee. And guess what? He only wears one pair of pants—at least, in the last three days he has. The first day I noticed the hole. The next day, I saw the same hole, and the next day as well. When I thought about it more, I realized that Nathan pretty much wore the same pants every single day during the entire school year!

4. On top of that, I also realized that Nathan only has two or three T-shirts and wears them over and over and over again.

5. Uncle Jake asked me what kind of backpack Nathan has. But there was a problem with that one, because Nathan doesn't have a backpack.

He carries his stuff in an old plastic grocery bag, and not just his snacks—everything.

6. And for snacks, Nathan must not get very hungry during camp, because he never brings much to snack on. Over the past three days, he only brought a snack one time—and it wasn't much of a snack at all. It was just a plastic bag with some potato chips in it.

Not really
that happy

Doesn't get to
washing his hair

Plastic bag from
the grocery store

His clothes
have holes

So after three days, I told Uncle Jake all I had learned about Nathan. I told him that he was dirty, didn't eat healthy foods, and was too lazy to even change clothes!

"Is that what you think, Marc?" Uncle Jake asked me.

"Well, YES!" I answered. "Of course! If he doesn't want to be dirty, why won't he change clothes? If he isn't lazy, why doesn't he get a backpack to carry his gear around in? And if he wants to eat healthy foods, why does he just bring potato chips to school?" It all made perfect sense to me.

"Maybe he doesn't have money for new clothes. Maybe he can't afford a new backpack. And maybe he doesn't have any healthy food at home so that he can fix himself healthy snacks for the day. Did you ever think about that, Marc?"

I certainly had not thought about that. "No, Uncle Jake. Not really."

"Okay. Well, think about it now: Maybe Nathan and his family don't have the money to buy new clothes, get a new backpack, or have good food. You don't know. And if they can't afford good clothes, do you think they can afford a nice house? A car? Video games and TVs and a big garage with a gym in it? And jiu-jitsu lessons? There is a chance that they can't afford much of anything. And how do you think that would make a person feel? How would it make *you* feel?"

"Not good, Uncle Jake."

"That's right, Marc. Not good. That's why we gather

intelligence. So we know what the problem is. Maybe Nathan has more problems in his life than just having a big mouth and being annoying."

"Maybe," I said as I thought about all the nice things I have. "Maybe."

"All right. Well, we will gather some more intelligence soon. Until then, keep your cool."

"Yes, Uncle Jake," I told him. "I will."

Uncle Jake walked out of the room, and I changed into my pajamas. My nice, clean pajamas. And I wondered to myself if Nathan even had pajamas. . . .

Probably not.

CHAPTER 13: CONSISTENCY

"Well? What are you going to do?" Uncle Jake asked.

I knew he was going to ask me that. Today was the last day to sign up for the jiu-jitsu tournament—and Uncle Jake wasn't going to forget it.

Part of me had thought that if I just ignored it and didn't say anything, then maybe by the time Uncle Jake remembered the tournament, it would be too late to sign up.

I should have known better! Because it was the first thing Uncle Jake asked me about this morning!

But it was fine. I had been thinking about what Uncle Jake told me. I was afraid of losing, but Uncle Jake told me that being afraid of losing is okay. And even if I lose, I would learn.

But I was still nervous about it. "Can I tell you at the end of jiu-jitsu class tonight?"

"You are going to have to, because today is the last day to sign up for the tournament," Uncle Jake said.

"Okay. I will."

When I got to jiu-jitsu class, we warmed up, worked on some new moves, and then did some training.

In between drills, I talked to Nora. She's a year younger than me and is a lot smaller than I am, but she is REALLY GOOD at jiu-jitsu. She's been doing it for a long time—and she does all kinds of competitions. She asked me if I was going to enter the tournament.

"Are you doing it?" I asked her.

"Of course I am!" she said without any hesitation at all. It was kind of amazing. Here was Nora, younger than me and smaller than me, and yet she wasn't afraid AT ALL. "Are you?" she asked again.

"Well . . . I'm thinking about it. . . ."

"Thinking about it? What is there to think about?" she said.

"Well . . . you know . . . training . . . and, you know . . . preparation . . . that kind of stuff. . . ."

"Training and preparation? What do you think we do in here every day? Every time we train, we are preparing to compete!"

She did have a good point there. Finally, I got up the

courage to ask her if she was scared. Only I didn't use the word *scared*. I used the word *nervous*. I think I was scared to use the word *scared*!

"Do you get nervous?"

"Of course I get a little nervous," Nora said, "but we do jiu-jitsu all the time, so there isn't too much to get nervous about. It's like training, only everyone tries really hard. But other than that, it's just jiu-jitsu. There isn't anything to be nervous about."

"What about losing? Don't you get nervous that you might lose?"

"'Might lose'? I've lost plenty of times!"

"What about all those medals and trophies you have won?" I asked. There were pictures all over the academy of Nora with trophies and medals.

"Sure, I won those times. But there have been plenty of times when I lost, too. I don't have pictures of those times, but I have lost more than I have won. Especially when I first started competing."

"And you don't mind losing?"

"I don't like it. But I don't mind it, either. I know that if I don't compete, I can never win. That is *really* losing!"

Here was a fifth-grade girl telling me almost the exact same thing as Uncle Jake. That's it! I was going to compete!

"That's what I think, too," I told her, wanting to sound a little tougher than I was. "That is why I am going to do this tournament!"

"Awesome. It will be fun," she said.

After that, I trained really hard for the rest of class. REALLY HARD.

Every time I sparred someone, I imagined myself competing in the tournament at the end of the summer. I tried not to give up any positions, and I tried to get everyone I trained with to tap out. By the end of class, I was sweating pretty hard.

Uncle Jake came in to pick me up from class.

"Well?" he said.

"Yes, Uncle Jake. I'm going to compete." As soon as I said those words, I felt kind of different. I felt nervous, but at the same time, I felt kind of good.

"That's what I like to hear," Uncle Jake told me. "You will get a lot out of it. You'll see."

When we got home, Uncle Jake came out to the garage with me and helped me do some work on my old, rusty bike. Actually, the bike wasn't that rusty anymore. The rims looked great, the handlebars were done, and the frame was about halfway cleaned up.

I may have to go into the bike-fixing business!

"It's starting to look pretty good, isn't it, Marc?" Uncle Jake asked me.

"It is. I never thought it could look like this again. And it doesn't seem like it's taken that much time."

"That's the way it is supposed to feel. But if you think about it, you have probably worked on this bike for twenty hours."

"You think so?"

"I know so. You have been working on it for over a month for a half hour to an hour at a time. So yes—it's been at least twenty hours of work so far."

"It doesn't feel like that much," I told Uncle Jake.

"That's because you broke it down and maintained consistency."

"Maintained what?" I asked.

"*Consistency*. You see, instead of trying to do this whole big project at one time, you just put in a little work here and there, chipping away at it each day. That way it didn't feel like a ton of work. And yet you look up now and can see all the progress you have made."

"Yeah. It really hasn't seemed like too much. Even though there were some nights when I didn't want to do it."

DISCIPLINE EQUALS FREEDOM

"You didn't want to, but you did. That makes the difference. That's discipline. You know, that's what I did in college this year. When I would get a big assignment,

I would work on it a little bit each day. Just for an hour or so. In a week, I had done seven hours. In two weeks, I was about done and had time to review and revise my work. Some of the other students wouldn't start their assignments until a couple of days before they were due. Then they would be scrambling to get them done and wouldn't be able to turn in their best work. And they would have to work fifteen hours straight on one thing—which can get boring. So that is what you do whenever you can: You break down big projects into small chunks and work on them a little bit every day."

"It's like cleaning my room, too."

"Really?"

"Yes. If I clean my room every day, it only takes a few minutes each time. But when I don't clean it for a week, all of a sudden it takes an hour to clean!"

"Exactly. Now, you'll also have to remember that there will be times when you don't have a choice. Sometimes you just have to focus and work on something for a long time. Like if you get a project late or something unexpected happens. One time when I was on a trip, my water heater broke, flooded my apartment, and ruined the floor. When I got home, I had to pull out the old floor and put a new one in, all before my next trip. I worked thirty-six straight hours to get that done. So even though a warrior likes to plan things out and break them down into small pieces, you don't always get that option."

"But if I have the option, I should plan, break it down into pieces, and do it in small chunks, right?"

"Exactly. Now, let's go get some dinner," Uncle Jake said.

"Okay."

"Malt Shoppe?" he asked, knowing I would definitely want to go to my favorite restaurant.

"YES!" I said, immediately thinking of some FOOD!

CHAPTER 14: LAZY DAY

I seem to learn something new all the time when Uncle Jake is here. Today I learned a very important lesson.

It all started on Friday. I woke up early, worked out with Uncle Jake, went to camp until lunch, came home, did chores for my mom, went to the academy, trained SUPER HARD in jiu-jitsu, got home, worked on my bike, ate dinner, and then went to bed. I was EXHAUSTED, and as soon as I lay down in bed, I fell asleep immediately.

Almost as soon as my head hit the pillow, my alarm was going off and it was time to get up and do it again. I know MOST kids relax on Saturdays, but, in case you didn't notice, Warrior Kids don't get much time to relax! So I got up, did burpees FOREVER with Uncle Jake, and then got to work—it was time to pull weeds and mow lawns, and I did it all weekend long.

I also got another lovely and enjoyable new job. Last week, I asked Mr. Latham down the street if there was anything he needed from me. The thing is, Mr. Latham doesn't have any real yard. Well, he has a yard, but in his yard, nothing grows. NOTHING. His whole yard is concrete and pavement. There is no grass and no flowers and no trees and not even any weeds to pull. Not a thing! But since I am a motivated young business owner, I figured that I would see if there was anything he did need. Last weekend he said no. I should have never gone back! But I did.

I went by his house again on Saturday morning and asked if there was anything I could do to help him. He immediately said, "Yes, there is! Come on over here, boy." He led me through his house and out his back door.

His backyard was the same as the front yard—all concrete and pavement, and there was a giant concrete patio, which was dyed a reddish color. It all actually looked pretty nice except one thing: There was a big, dirty, whitish-gray stain going diagonally across the ENTIRE PATIO.

"You see that over there, kid?" he said to me, pointing to the giant stain. "That's bird guano."

I wasn't sure what he was talking about.

"'Guano'?" I said.

"Yes, boy. *Guano.* You know what guano is?"

"No, sir," I told him.

"Droppings, boy! Bird droppings!"

Now I was really confused. What do birds drop? So I asked him. "What do birds drop?"

"You aren't as smart as you look, kid," Mr. Latham said. "It's poo. Bird poo. All of it. They sit up on that wire there and poo all over my patio!"

He pointed up above the patio. There was a wire running from the alley that went above his yard and to his roof. And, sure enough, there were some birds sitting on it. And yes, while we were looking up, one of them pooed right on the patio!

"Now, I'm getting that wire removed next week, but right now I need all this poop off my patio. And I think you are the man to do the job."

This DID NOT LOOK LIKE FUN. Cleaning bird poo for a living! So I quickly made some excuses. "I'm sorry, Mr. Latham, but I'm more of a yard work kind of guy."

"This is my yard," he replied.

I needed to think quickly. "I know, Mr. Latham. But the problem is that I only have tools for a regular yard. I don't have the right kinds of tools for this type of job, but I appreciate the offer." *Perfect*, I thought. *That was the perfect excuse.*

At least, I thought it was until Mr. Latham said, "Don't worry, kid. I have all the tools you need: a scrub brush, gloves, water, and a bucket. Come on. I'll take you to them and show you the hose."

My excuse making was done. *Oh well*, I thought. Like Uncle Jake told me, I would make money doing jobs that other people don't want to do. And NO ONE would want to do this job.

"Yes, sir," I said as I followed him over to his toolshed. He handed me a big bucket, a small hand brush, and a pair of rubber gloves. Then he showed me where the hose was. I filled up the bucket with water.

"There you go, kid. Let me know if you need anything else."

"Yes, sir," I said. And with that, I got down on my knees and started scrubbing. And scrubbing. And scrubbing! It took hours and hours—five hours to be precise—of me, on my hands and knees, scrubbing bird poop! By the time I was done, the patio looked perfect. I hosed the whole thing down, put the bucket, gloves, and scrub brush away, and knocked on Mr. Latham's door. He came outside, walked across the patio, and looked at it from a bunch of different angles. Finally he announced, "This looks great, kid," and he took out his wallet and handed me two twenty-dollar bills—forty dollars!

That made me feel great . . . for about two minutes. Then I remembered that I still had work to do at other houses. So I went around to my other appointments: the Jacksons, the Kirths, and the Newsomes. I mowed and pulled weeds as quickly as I could. But I still worked until six o'clock. When I got home, I ate a quick dinner and then worked on my bike. When I was done with that, I went to bed, EXHAUSTED once again!

The next day was a repeat—minus the bird poo. I was up early in the morning to work out, then immediately

went to houses pulling weeds and mowing lawns. And it was HOT, so it was even more tiring than normal. Once again, I got home, ate a quick dinner, and went out to the garage to work on my bike.

I couldn't wait to get to bed, but then I suddenly remembered that there was no camp the next day. I decided I would take the day off from doing ANYTHING! That's right! I needed a day of rest.

When I was done working on my bike, I walked back to the house. Uncle Jake was sitting at the table, reading a book. I knew he wasn't going to like this, but I also knew that if I didn't say something, tomorrow would be just as much work as today.

"Uncle Jake?" I said.

"What's up, Marc?" he replied as he looked up from his book.

"I'm really tired."

"That's great. It means you had a productive day filled with hard work. Good job."

"No, Uncle Jake. I mean I'm REALLY tired. And tomorrow I don't have camp, and, well, I was just wondering if it would be okay if I took the day off and did NOTHING."

"Nothing? No workout? No work on your bike? No work. You sure about that?"

"I am, Uncle Jake. I'm just really tired." I was waiting for Uncle Jake to tell me that this was a bad idea, or that I needed to push through it, or that I needed to take advantage of every day I have or something like that.

Instead he just said, "Okay."

And that was it. He went back to reading.

YIPPEEE! DAY OFF!

So I went upstairs and turned off my alarm clock

and put on my pajamas and went to bed. The next morning I woke up early, but since it was my day off, I just stayed in bed for a while.

I saw Uncle Jake when I came down for breakfast. He was already done working out and said he had to go to the library to do some research, and my mom had already left for some kind of event she had for work.

It was perfect! As soon as Uncle Jake left, I sat down on the couch and watched some TV. Then I got on the computer and watched some videos. Then I played some games on the computer. When I was done with that, I watched some more TV.

Uncle Jake got home in the afternoon with some books he had borrowed from the library. Then he put on some workout clothes, grabbed a backpack, and said he was going to go out for a while.

So I watched some *more* TV and played some *more* games on the computer and then I watched some *more* videos! SWEET!

Uncle Jake came home just before dinner. He was all dirty-looking and sweaty.

We sat down to eat.

"So how was your day off? What did you do?" Uncle Jake asked me.

"Not much really. Just relaxed, I guess."

"Oh. Sounds like TV and video games."

"Yeah. Some," I told Uncle Jake, knowing that he knew what that really meant—that I had watched a TON of TV and played a TON of video games.

"What about you? What did you do?"

"I did a bunch of research at the library. I'm learning more about the First World War. Then I wrote a dozen or so e-mails to friends of mine. Guys all over the world. Then I worked on the design of a house I'm going to build one day. When I was done with that, I went rock climbing, which was awesome. So it was a good day."

GUESS WHO'S PUMPED TO CRUSH HIS GOALS?

THIS UNCLE!!

Rock climbing! Designing houses! Researching World War I! I felt like I missed out on a lot of good stuff. "Sheesh, Uncle Jake! I didn't know you were doing all that good stuff today! I wish I could have done some of it with you."

"You could have. But it was your day off. And speaking of your day off, how does it feel?"

"What do you mean?"

"I mean the day off that you said you needed so bad. How was it? Did you enjoy it?"

"Well." I wasn't sure what to say, but I wanted to stay positive, so I said, "Yes." The problem was that I didn't even believe that. It wasn't an enjoyable day. So I changed my answer. "Kind of," I told him. But I knew that wasn't true, either—the day wasn't even *kind of* enjoyable. So I changed my answer again. "I mean, I guess." But now I just felt that he didn't believe me anyway, so I told him, "Maybe not." But there shouldn't have even been a *maybe*. The day was not good, and I knew it. So finally, I told the truth, "No, Uncle Jake. No, I didn't have a good day."

"Why not?"

"I don't know. I guess I just didn't do much. I mean, I did some stuff, but . . . you know, it was just kind of . . . just kind of . . ."

"Lazy. You had a lazy day," Uncle Jake said. He knew it!

"Yes, Uncle Jake. It was lazy. I thought I needed it. I thought it would feel good!"

"Of course you did. Lazy days always feel good when you start them. But the problem comes when they are done. When they are done, they never feel good. You never look back at a lazy day and say, 'I'm glad that I didn't do anything today! I'm glad I didn't make any progress! I'm glad I didn't accomplish anything!' No. Why would you say that? It would never be true. But lazy days are tempting when you are facing the hard work, before you have started. Or when you are tired and you want that easy day. Once it's done, the lazy day never feels good."

Uncle Jake was right again. Even though it seemed like I needed it and it seemed like it would feel good, the fact of the matter is that, at the end of the day, it didn't feel good. I accomplished nothing today. And the worst part was that I didn't even feel refreshed! I actually felt just as tired, if not MORE TIRED, from sitting around all day than I would have felt if I'd gone after it!

"No, Uncle Jake. It doesn't."

After a quiet minute or two, Uncle Jake looked at me and said, "Well, you know what you did accomplish today?"

"No, Uncle Jake. What?"

"You learned. You learned that laziness is never the right path. And that is a good lesson, because you can't get a lazy day back. They are gone forever. Don't ever forget that, Marc."

"I won't, Uncle Jake. I won't."

Uncle Jake nodded. He knew I wouldn't.

I went upstairs and got ready for bed, excited for my opportunity to have a great day tomorrow.

CHAPTER 15: A DIFFERENT WORLD

I learned some things today that I'd never thought about before. And I think they will make me a better person.

Uncle Jake told me we were going on a mission and he was going to pick me up after camp. When I got out of camp, he was standing on the street across from the rec center. He motioned me over, and I walked toward him. When I got close to him, he asked, "Without pointing, which kid is Nathan?"

I looked back toward the rec center and saw Nathan. "There he is, over there."

"You have to be more specific. What color shirt? What color pants? Where is he standing?"

"Okay. He is wearing a black T-shirt and black jeans, and he has black hair. He's standing by the flagpole."

"Got him. Okay. Track him. We're walking down the street."

With that, Uncle Jake and I walked down to the end of the street and took a left. Then he sat down on a bench on the sidewalk and told me to have a seat, too.

"What are we doing?" I asked Uncle Jake.

"Some more *reconnaissance*—another word for gathering intelligence—and surveillance. We are going to watch Nathan and learn some more about him. Keep an eye on him."

"Okay," I told Uncle Jake. I wasn't sure why we needed to do this, but it seemed like a pretty cool thing.

So we sat and watched. And watched. And watched some more.

And Nathan stayed there, hanging around the flagpole while other kids got picked up or jumped on their bikes and went home. After a while, the last kid and even all the camp counselors left. Once everyone was gone, Nathan hung around for a while on his own. Then, finally, he walked down the street, heading toward town.

As he walked, it didn't even seem like he was going anywhere. We stood up and walked pretty far behind him so he wouldn't notice us, but we could still see him. He would stop and look at things. He would pick things up off the ground, look at them for a while, and then either put them in his pocket or toss them back on the ground. He would do little tricks or stunts on benches or curbs or stairs, jumping on them and off them or over them, doing spins or kicks or waving his arms. Sometimes he would stop in front of houses and just look at them for a while.

We would stop every so often to hide behind something so Nathan wouldn't see us. Then, every time Nathan would almost leave our vision, Uncle Jake would start walking again. We would get a little closer, then stop somewhere behind him or maybe duck into a side street, where we could still see him.

After a while, Nathan finally seemed to get where he was going: the parking lot of the Quickie Mart store. When Nathan got there, he went over to a little tree, hung the plastic bag that he'd been carrying in the branches, and sat down on the curb, leaning up against the tree trunk. It seemed like he had done this before.

When some people would walk in and out of the store, Nathan would say hi to them, like he knew them.

One of the people went in the store, and when they came back out, they gave Nathan a hot dog. Another person that Nathan talked to for a minute came out of the store and handed Nathan a can of soda. Other people just said hi to him and then carried on. Occasionally, people would hand him empty cans or bottles that they had in their cars.

It was very strange.

Nathan stayed there for a long time, sitting on the curb. He folded up the wrapper of his hot dog about ten different ways. Once he finished the can of soda, he tore off part of the hot dog wrapper, made it into a little ball, and then started trying to throw it into the can, like a miniature game of basketball. Every time he "scored," he made a new little ball and started throwing that one, too.

When people handed him cans or plastic bottles, he would crush them and put them into his plastic bag, hanging in the tree. Finally, after a pretty long time, Nathan grabbed his bag, waved to the store cashier through the window, and walked down the street.

We followed him once again. This time he stopped at a grocery store. He went in with his bag packed full of bottles and cans and walked back out a few minutes later with the bag empty.

"He just turned in those cans for recycling. He might have made a dollar or two," Uncle Jake said.

Once he was done turning in his recycling, he looked through the garbage cans at the grocery store and found a few more bottles. He also went and talked to some of the people who pulled up in cars. We couldn't hear him because we were standing in a store across the street, but he must have been asking for cans or bottles, because sometimes people would give them to him.

Don't judge. Everyone has to make a living.

After he gathered up some more cans and bottles, he went back into the grocery store. This time he came out with a little ready-made sandwich that he ate while sitting on a bench.

"Looks like he has to work to get his food," Uncle Jake said. It sure did.

Once Nathan finished his sandwich, he was on the move once more. Again, it didn't seem like he was heading anywhere fast. He took his time, stopping and fidgeting with things, looking at things, picking things up and tossing them.

He walked for a pretty long ways, through downtown and past all the stores, some of which he went into. Then he walked out to the other side of town and over the railroad tracks, to where there weren't houses anymore but warehouses and little run-down stores and places where there were car repair shops and welding shops. Some of the places looked pretty rough.

We continued to follow Nathan from a couple of blocks away.

Nathan would stop by some of the shops. I could tell he must do this every day, because the people in the

shops recognized him and said hi. Sometimes he would come out of the shops carrying a half-empty bag of potato chips or maybe a part of a cookie.

"Well, now we know where Nathan gets his meals," Uncle Jake said.

"I guess so," I replied. But I hadn't really thought about that. In fact, in my mind it seemed kinda cool that he was getting all this food from people. But when Uncle Jake said that, I realized that it wasn't cool AT ALL. This is where Nathan *had* to get his food.

Finally, Nathan got to a building that he stopped in front of. The building was made of brick, but it was really run-down. Outside was a sign that said LEM'S METAL WORKS. There was a door off to the side of that. Nathan reached into his pocket and pulled out a key. He opened the door and disappeared inside. A few seconds later, we saw a light come on upstairs. It was pretty obvious that he was home alone.

"Come on, Marc, let's go," Uncle Jake said as he motioned with his head to start walking away and back toward the rec center. By this time, it was really late and really dark. It was definitely past my bedtime. "Seems like his life is a lot different than yours, doesn't it?" he asked.

"Yes, Uncle Jake. It sure does."

"What kind of kid do you think you would be if that

was your life? Do you think you would be as nice as you are? Do you think you would be a little jealous of other kids, with their nice snacks packed for them every day and the nice houses they live in?"

"Probably, Uncle Jake," I told him. He was right. "It almost seems like Nathan lives in a totally different world than me."

"That's because he *does* live in a totally different world than you. Now, do you think that if you lived in that world—where you were alone most of the time and basically begging for food—do you think you might have a hard time relating to kids that have everything given to them? Do you think you might even be mean to them?"

I thought about that for a second. "Just because he doesn't have nice food doesn't give him the right to be mean to people," I told Uncle Jake.

"I didn't say that it gave him the right," replied Uncle Jake, "but do you see how it could happen? Do you understand maybe why Nathan might act the way he does?"

Uncle Jake was right. Nathan's life seemed A LOT tougher than mine. And while I didn't think that gave him the right to be mean, I could see how it might make him mean—especially to kids who seemed so spoiled in comparison to him . . . LIKE ME!

"I do understand it, Uncle Jake," I said.

"Okay. So. Now, instead of wanting to fight Nathan, maybe you should think about how you can help him. How you can change him for the better. How you can *lead* him. Fighting him would be the simple thing to do. It would be the easy path. Actually *helping* him would be tougher. But it would be the right thing to do. That's what warriors do. We do the right thing, even if it is harder."

"But how can I help him? I can't change his life."

"You don't have to change his life, but maybe you can point him in the right direction."

Uncle Jake got quiet for a minute as we finally turned down the street to our house. "Remember what you were like before you got on the war- rior path? Before you became a Warrior Kid?"

"Yes! I was a wimp!"

"Okay. Well, guess what? The warrior path doesn't only help wimpy kids. It can help any kid. Even kids like Nathan. He could use discipline and focus in his life. It would only make his life—and him—better, which would also make him nicer."

Uncle Jake was right again, but there was one big problem. "That all sounds great, Uncle Jake, but here is the big question: How? How am I supposed to do this? I can't make him change. I can't force him to be a different person."

"You're right, Marc. You can't. You can't force people to change. You can't force people to be different. That doesn't work."

"So what am I supposed to do?" I asked Uncle Jake.

LIFE CHANGING'S
ABOVE MY PAY
GRADE.

"There is only one way: You have to *lead.*"

With that, we quietly went into the house without saying a word so we wouldn't wake my mom up.

So that's it, I thought as I lay in bed. *I have to lead.*

CHAPTER 16: THE REAL PLATE FACE

Today was different.

During my workout this morning with Uncle Jake, I asked him how I was supposed to lead Nathan. I couldn't just walk up to him and say, "Do what I tell you!" That wouldn't work. Uncle Jake agreed.

"That definitely won't work," Uncle Jake said. "That kind of leadership isn't real leadership. Sure, if you were in charge of someone and you ordered them to do something, that might work at first. But it won't last. Real leadership comes by forming relationships with people—by becoming friends with people. Then they will listen to you because they *want* to—not because they *have* to."

"So I have to become friends with Nathan?"

"Well, you are at least going to have to try."

This isn't going quite the way I hoped . . .

"How am I going to be friends with someone who makes fun of me every chance he gets?" I asked Uncle

Jake. I was starting to suspect that maybe he hadn't thought his idea all the way through!

Uncle Jake then asked me, "Has he ever punched you?"

This was a strange question. "No," I told Uncle Jake.

"What about kicked? Has he ever kicked you?"

"No, Uncle Jake. He has never kicked me."

"What about slapped or scratched or bit you?"

"No. He hasn't."

"Okay, then, Marc. What has he done to you?"

This question had me quiet for a minute. What had Nathan done to me? I could barely remember when it all started. "Well, he makes fun of me. He calls me names."

"Oh yeah, that's right," Uncle Jake said, smiling. "Plate Face."

"That's not funny, Uncle Jake," I told him.

"Well. Maybe you don't think so. But it is kind of funny."

"Not really," I told him again.

"You might think it was funny if you didn't take it so seriously. Think about it. Your face is a little roundish. And a little flat. Like a plate. So 'Plate Face.' If you just let it be funny, you would see that it *is* funny. But you are being too sensitive about it. A warrior can't let a little name-calling upset them. Warriors have more important things to be concerned about—things that matter. Someone making fun of you or calling you a name isn't important enough. Just deal with it and move on."

"Okay, but it annoys me. How do I 'just deal with it'?"

"That's the easy part. You just laugh. Laugh! Laugh along with the joke. Instead of getting mad, just think of it from a different perspective and LAUGH. And here is another secret: Not only will laughing make you feel better, it will also take away the power of the insult. People make fun of other people to feel powerful. As soon as you laugh at yourself, you take that power away from them. Try it. You will see."

"Okay, Uncle Jake, I'll try it."

The next day at camp, after kickball in the morning, we had an art project to do. I figured that this was as good a time as any to try and make friends with Nathan, so I sat at the same table as him. I think this kind of surprised him, because he looked at me in a strange way for a minute. There wasn't much time to talk, because we were doing individual projects. As soon as we sat down, the counselor told us to be quiet and start listening. The counselor said we were going to draw a *self-portrait*, which is a picture of yourself.

As soon as I heard this, I had an idea—an idea that would help me become friends with Nathan and help me laugh at myself.

So I drew a picture of myself. But instead of drawing myself the way I actually look, I drew myself as "Plate Face!" I made my face a giant plate, with my hair and eyes but in the shape of a PLATE! Then I added a little body, which made it look even funnier.

When I finished it, I whispered to Nathan, "Hey, Nathan, check this out. . . ." I held up the picture.

Nathan burst out laughing! When he started laughing so hard, I started laughing, too. It was hilarious!!!

"The real Plate Face!" I told him.

"That's awesome!" he said back. "You're a great artist . . . because that looks just like you!!" We started laughing even harder.

And that was it. I no longer felt bad about being called Plate Face, and Nathan could tell that it didn't bother me anymore.

"I didn't know you were so funny, Marc!" he said. That was it. He called me Marc. That must have been the first time he called me by my real name in a year.

But more important, it now seemed like I had a new friend.

CHAPTER 17: THE BRUISER

Today was AWESOME. After all the taking apart and cleaning and removing rust and sanding and preparing for paint and painting each individual part with two or three coats of paint, it was FINALLY time to put my rust-bucket bike back together again. Only now it didn't look like a rust bucket. In fact, there was no rust on it at all! Every part looked almost brand-new. I say *almost*, because instead of being all new and shiny, this bike was almost completely black!

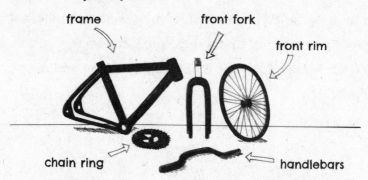

frame   front fork   front rim

chain ring   handlebars

I actually wasn't feeling very comfortable about putting the bike together by myself, and I think Uncle Jake knew that, so he came to the garage to help me out. Well, at least I thought he was there to help me.

"Thanks for coming to help me," I told him.

"'Help' you?"

"Well, yeah," I said. "I thought you were here to help me out?"

"I'm here to answer any questions you might have. I'm here to make sure you aren't making any mistakes. But you are the one who has to do the work," Uncle Jake said.

"Okay. Well. Thanks, I guess."

"You 'guess'?" Uncle Jake laughed. "Why do you only 'guess'?"

"Well," I told him, "why should I thank you if you aren't even going to help me?" I asked Uncle Jake this with a smile on my face. He knew I was teasing him, and he could tell that I thought it was pretty funny. I thought he did, too, until his face got serious.

"If I help you, I'm hurting you," he said, staring right at me.

"What?"

"I said, 'If I help you, I'm hurting you.'"

"I heard what you said, Uncle Jake. But what does that even mean? How can you be hurting me if you help me?" This idea seemed kind of crazy to me!

But it wasn't crazy to Uncle Jake, and I could see it in his eyes. "Here's the thing, Marc. One of the best ways for people to learn is by *doing*. If I were to jump in and put the bike back together myself, you wouldn't learn anything. If you don't learn, what is the point? That's why I always want you to do things yourself—so you can learn to be self-sufficient. So you don't need help. Of course, there are some things that you will need help with in life, and putting this bike together right now is one of them. Sometimes someone needs to show you how to do things and guide you through them. But whenever you can, try to do them yourself so you learn. Does that make sense?"

"Yes, Uncle Jake. It does. If I can put this bike together with very little help from you, then in the future maybe I won't need any help at all."

"That's right," Uncle Jake said. "You will be able to take care of yourself. You will be self-sufficient. It will be awesome. Now what you need to do is stop talking and get to work! Start with putting the seat in and then put the stem back in the frame so you can put the handlebars on. Then you can flip it over and it will be stable so you can start putting the back cranks on."

"Got it, Uncle Jake."

With that, I picked up the frame, fed the stem through the neck, and started tightening it down. Uncle Jake helped a little by holding the frame steady. After that I put the seat on, then the cranks, which were a little bit tricky. I almost needed Uncle Jake's help again but managed to get it done. Then I had to put the tubes and tires on the rims so they would be ready to go on the bike.

As I put each piece back on the bike, it started looking even better and better than when I began working on it. Each piece fit into place nicely.

Finally, it was time to put the tires on the bike, get the chain in place, attach the brakes, and, last step, pump up the tires with air. Once I finished, that was it. It looked AMAZING. Almost the whole bike was black, and it looked like a bike that could be used for Warrior Kid missions!

"Looks pretty good," Uncle Jake said.

"'Pretty good'?" I said. "It looks AWESOME!"

Uncle Jake looked at the bike for a few seconds, then said, "Hold on. It is missing something."

With that, he walked out of the garage. A minute later, he came back in. He had a small bag in his hand. He reached inside, pulled out a little packet, and handed it to me. I looked at the little packet. It was a bunch of little sticker letters.

"You need to name it," Uncle Jake said.

"'Name it'?"

"Yeah. Give it a name. That bike you used to want was named The Bentlee. You need to name this bike something."

"What should I name it?"

"I don't know. What does it remind you of? What did The Bentlee remind you of?"

"Well, The Bentlee is all shiny and nice. It doesn't look as tough as this bike."

"So you want a name that is tough?"

"Yeah. The toughest. This is the toughest bike. It needs the toughest name."

"That sounds like a good plan. So what is the toughest name?"

"Good question," I replied. I sat there for a minute,

thinking. What was the toughest name? Then I remembered Uncle Jake telling me a story about a really tough group of SEALs he worked with that fought super hard against the enemy. And I remembered what they were called. BRUISER.

"What about The Bruiser?" I said. "Like that group of SEALs you said you worked with."

Uncle Jake smiled and nodded his head. "The Bruiser. I like it. And I think it fits perfectly. Go ahead," he said as he pointed to the stickers.

I pulled out the stickers and started to peel of the *T* to get started.

"Hold on," Uncle Jake said. "First, figure out exactly where you want to put it. Then take this ruler and draw a straight line with the pencil so it looks professional."

I did as instructed and then I peeled off the *T* and put it in place. It looked good, so I followed with the rest of the letters. Once I was done, I stepped back and had a look.

It read THE BRUISER. The bike looked EVEN BETTER NOW. IT WAS AWESOME.

I got on the other side of the bike, drew a line, and put the stickers on that side, too. DOUBLE AWESOME!!

"Well," Uncle Jake said, "hopefully you can sell it for enough money to get The Bentlee."

"What?!?!" I shouted. "The Bentlee? Why would I want The Bentlee now?!"

Uncle Jake had a big smile on his face. "Well, I haven't even seen The Bentlee, but I don't think it can be any better than The Bruiser!"

"NO WAY!" I shouted. "NOT EVEN CLOSE!!!"

"'Not even close,'" Uncle Jake said. "That's what happens when you do the work—when you build something yourself with your own hands. It is really YOURS. Good job, Marc."

"Thanks, Uncle Jake. Thanks for making me do the work."

"No problem, Marc," he said. "No problem at all."

Then he pushed the button to open the garage door, handed me my helmet, and sent me out on my first ride.

And IT WAS AWESOME!

CHAPTER 18: IT REALLY WORKS

I rode The Bruiser to camp today! It was FUN and FAST! When I got to camp, I showed the bike to Nathan. He asked me who made The Bruiser bike. I told him ME! He was super excited about it and told me it looked like a SERIOUS MACHINE! I even let him take a ride around the rec center before camp started, and he said it rode like a RACE CAR!

After camp started, Nathan and I headed to the classroom for another art session. Today we were making a bridge with straws, tape, and toothpicks. The bridge had to reach across eighteen inches and be able to hold a five-pound weight at its middle point. It was pretty cool. Whichever team built their bridge the fastest—and passed the test—was the winner.

We were the third-fastest team, but the team that got it done the fastest had some big problems when the weight was placed on their bridge—the whole thing collapsed! So we ended up in second place, which wasn't too bad.

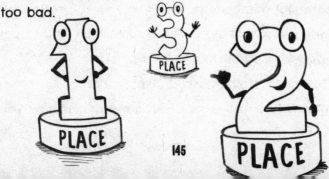

It turns out Nathan is a pretty cool kid now that I am getting to know him.

It seems like he was interested in a lot of things I do but didn't want to ask about them before. Today he asked me about jiu-jitsu.

"So what is the deal with that jiu-jitsu stuff you do? Is it some kind of karate?"

JIU-JITSU IS AMAZING!

"No, not really. Jiu-jitsu doesn't use punches and kicks like karate and a lot of other martial arts do."

"Well, how can you ever win a fight without punching or kicking? Isn't that what fighting is?"

"Punching and kicking aren't the only form of fighting. Jiu-jitsu is more like a form of wrestling. You use moves to get dominant positions on your opponent. But then you use something called a submission hold to get your opponent to tap out."

"'Tap out'?" Nathan asked. "What's that?"

"That is how you give up in jiu-jitsu. It is how you

surrender. When someone gets you in a hold that could do some real damage, like an armlock or a choke, then you just tap them a few times until they let go."

"And that's it?"

"Well, in practice that's it. That's why it's called practice or training. You and your opponent are not trying to hurt each other. You are just trying to get to the position where you *could*. Once you get caught there, you tap out. If you are the one that catches someone in a submission hold, you hold it until they tap out. But you don't ever put too much pressure to where you might actually hurt them. Unless it is a real self-defense situation, then you could apply more pressure and really hurt someone in order to protect yourself."

"And you really think this stuff would work?"

"I know it works, because I use it every day. That is the thing with jiu-jitsu: You really use it when you practice. Of course, you don't actually hurt anyone, but you do get them to the point where they have to give up. Then they tap. So it is like a real fight, but no one gets hurt."

"It sounds pretty cool!"

"It is pretty cool." Just as I finished saying that, I remembered that I had jiu-jitsu that night, and I decided it would be great if Nathan could come and learn some, too. "Do you want to try some this afternoon? I have class at four o'clock."

"I would, but . . . well . . ."

"'Well' what? Come on! You will like it."

"But . . . I mean . . . how much does it cost?"

I hadn't even thought of that. Uncle Jake and I had already seen that Nathan and his family didn't have much money. Luckily, my jiu-jitsu academy lets people come their first time for free.

"Don't worry about that right now. At the jiu-jitsu academy, the first class is free."

"That's cool. I definitely want to give it a try!" Nathan said with a big smile on his face.

That afternoon we picked up Nathan from the rec center and brought him to jiu-jitsu class. Once we were there, the instructor, Coach Adam, gave Nathan a *gi*–the uniform used in jiu-jitsu–to wear and invited him out onto the mat.

Then Coach Adam told me to teach the basics to Nathan. So I did. I showed him all the positions that we normally use in jiu-jitsu: mount, guard, half guard, full guard, across side, and, of course, the back mount. Then

I showed Nathan some of the techniques used to escape a mount. Finally, I showed him a couple of submission holds: first a really simple shoulder lock called the "Americana" and next a choke from the back called "Mata Leao," which means *lion killer.*

Each time I put the hold on and started to apply pressure, Nathan would tap and then say, "Do it again! Do it again!" So I would do it again and then with each move he would say, "Let me try it!"

Then I would talk him through the move on me, and he would do it to me. He couldn't believe how easily the moves worked and how simple it was to get someone to tap out if you knew the technique.

After a while, Coach Adam had us join with the rest of the class, and we worked on a couple more moves. Then when we were done with that, he set the class up for rolling and told me to train with Nathan.

Of course, even though Nathan knew the basics, he didn't know enough to do anything against me but tap out! Nathan looked a little frustrated that it was so easy to tap him out. But at the same time, I could see he was REALLY INTO IT.

I think Coach Adam wanted to prove that jiu-jitsu really works, and since I'm bigger than Nathan, Coach Adam had Nathan train with Nora, who is quite a bit smaller than Nathan. But that didn't matter, of course, since Nora knows jiu-jitsu. She was able to tap him out pretty easily, too.

When class was over, we walked down the stairs and Coach Adam gave Nathan a piece of paper that had the class schedule and the prices.

I watched Nathan's face fall when he saw how much it costs to train at the academy, and he looked pretty sad. We got in the car and didn't say much on the way back to the rec center to drop him off.

Once he got out of the car at the rec center and we drove away, Uncle Jake said, "Did you see Nathan's face when he saw how much the classes cost?"

"Yes, Uncle Jake."

"I don't think he can afford to pay that much."

"I don't, either," I told Uncle Jake.

"We will have to find another way, Marc."

"Another way?"

"Yes. Another way for Nathan to get money or a way for Nathan to pay."

I had no idea what this meant, but if it was coming from Uncle Jake, I was sure it meant something good.

CHAPTER 19: HELP

Today started off kind of weird. Not necessarily bad but just weird.

You see, when I was working out with Uncle Jake this morning, I told him something.

"I'm bored, Uncle Jake."

"Bored? How can you be bored? You're busy all day."

"That's the tricky thing. I know I'm busy all day with working out and mowing lawns and fixing my bike and going to summer camp and doing jiu-jitsu. But even with all that stuff going on, I still feel kind of bored. And I feel like I've done what I've wanted to do, so other than focusing on my jiu-jitsu tournament, I just feel, like . . . I don't know . . . bored."

Uncle Jake look at me for a few seconds and then said, "Good." That is what he always seemed to say when something was wrong.

"Good?" I asked. "How is that good?"

"Well, first of all, being bored means you're comfortable with what you have going on in your life. It is good for a few reasons. Number one, it means you have accomplished your goals. That means you have achieved what you wanted to achieve. You have a bike. You have made some money. You are making steady gains in your workouts and getting stronger. So that means you can set some new goals, like you have for jiu-jitsu. Now that you have the tournament coming up, you can focus on that. It makes it exciting. And you can do that for the rest of the things you are doing—find new goals. But the most important thing about being bored is that you have the *capacity*—and by that I mean the time, the money, the knowledge, and the willingness—to help other people. To help someone else. That is what a warrior should always strive to do. What is number five of your Warrior Kid Code?"

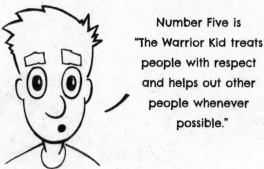

Number Five is "The Warrior Kid treats people with respect and helps out other people whenever possible."

"That is right," Uncle Jake said. "That is perfect. Warriors help other people *whenever possible*. Well, before, when you were struggling yourself, it wasn't possible for you to help other people. You had to help yourself first!

How could you teach things you didn't know? How could you share money you didn't have? How could you train someone else when you needed to be trained yourself? But all those things have changed now. You are a totally different person. Before, maybe you could help your mom clean the kitchen or help your dad clean the car. And even though those are nice things to do, now you can *really* help other people—you can have a legitimate impact on their lives."

"That sounds cool, Uncle Jake. But I'm not sure I get it. How can I help people in a big way?"

"There are all kinds of ways to help all kinds of people. But let's make this really simple. There is one person in your life that you can really help a lot right now. Who is it?"

Okay, I'm giving myself one guess. . . .

'Sup?

I knew exactly who Uncle Jake was talking about. "Nathan?"

"Yes. Nathan. He is a good kid, but he definitely faces a lot of challenges that you don't have to face. I'll tell you what: When we get done working out, go upstairs and write down three things that you can do to really help Nathan and then we will figure out how you can make them happen."

"Okay, Uncle Jake." So we finished up the workout (by doing one hundred burpees in a row!!) and then I went to my room, took out a piece of paper, and wrote down what Uncle Jake asked me to. When I was done, I went down and told Uncle Jake I was ready.

"What do you have?"

"Well, Uncle Jake. Here are the three things that I think Nathan could use some help with: First, he really liked jiu-jitsu class the other day, but I know he doesn't have enough money for it. Two, he doesn't have a bike. When he rode The Bruiser the other day, he looked so happy. But if he hasn't got enough money for jiu-jitsu class, then I'm sure he doesn't have enough money for a new bike. And finally, since Nathan doesn't seem to have much to do after camp every day, it seems like it would be really nice if he had a cool place to hang out."

"Okay. Those are good. I like those, and I agree. I

think those would be great ways to help Nathan. Now let's think about how we can actually accomplish them. But first things first—you have been working hard all summer to make money. Do you realize that we might have to spend some of that money to help Nathan? Are you okay with that?"

This was a tough question. Uncle Jake continued, "Before you answer that, understand that we are going to start by making sure *you* have money. That means taking twenty percent of what you've earned and putting it into savings. And that isn't just for now—that is always. You should always save twenty percent of your money. Then if there are other things you really need, you can buy those as well. And you should also know this: One of the few things in the world that feels better than earning money is earning money and then putting it toward a good cause to help someone else. I know that sounds strange, but it is true."

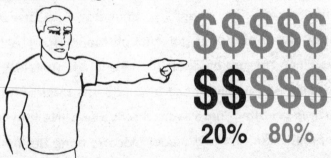

I wasn't sure how that could actually be true, but I

decided to listen to Uncle Jake since he always seemed to be right about everything.

"Okay, then, Uncle Jake. I will save twenty percent of my money, and if I think of anything else I really need, I will tell you. But if I need to spend some money to help Nathan, I will do that."

"All right. And I'll tell you what. Since you are being generous, I will be generous, too. Anything that we need to spend to help Nathan, I will give half of it so that you only have to give the other half."

"Thanks, Uncle Jake!" I told him, but then I realized I had no idea how we were ever going to do this, so I asked him, "But exactly what are we going to do?"

"Well, first off, for jiu-jitsu, we will go and talk to Coach Adam and see if he can give us a deal on the class price and if there is anything you and Nathan can do to help out around the academy. Next, we are going to buy a bike for Nathan."

"Buy him a bike? I don't have enough money for that!"

Uncle Jake laughed. "Don't worry, we aren't buying him a *new* bike. We can drive around and look for someone who is selling used bikes. We will buy a rust bucket—like your old bike—and then you and Nathan will repair and fix and paint it and put it all back together again."

"Awesome!"

"And while you two are refurbishing the bike, guess what?"

"What?"

"Nathan will have somewhere to go and something to do after camp every day. So that problem is solved, too."

"YES!" I shouted. "This plan is PERFECT!"

"Nope. There is no such thing as a perfect plan. And the plan doesn't happen if someone doesn't MAKE IT HAPPEN. So let's stop talking and get to work. We will start as soon as camp is over today by going to talk to Coach Adam."

"Got it, Uncle Jake."

This was awesome. And I was already realizing that Uncle Jake was right once again: It did feel good to help people.

CHAPTER 20: JUNKYARD

When I got home from camp today, Uncle Jake was waiting for me. He told me to grab all of my money, and we went straight from camp to Victory Mixed Martial Arts, where Coach Adam teaches jiu-jitsu. There was an adult class being taught, so we waited on the side of the mat for it to finish. When it was over, Uncle Jake told me to go talk to Coach Adam.

"Coach Adam, I have a question to ask."

"Sure, Marc. What is going on?"

"Well. You remember that kid I brought in the other day, with the black hair?"

"Oh, yeah . . . Nathan. He seemed like a really good kid. How did he like his first day of jiu-jitsu?"

"He loved it, Coach. He really did."

"That's great. It seemed like he liked it. Is he going to start training here all the time, like you do?"

So far, the conversation had been pretty easy. But this was the part I was nervous about. "Well, Coach, actually . . . he would love to start training here every single day, but the problem is that his family . . . well, they can't really afford to pay that much money. I was wondering if there was any way that he could train, well, maybe for free?"

Coach Adam sat quietly for a few seconds.

"Free?"

"Well, yeah. His family doesn't really have much money."

"And so you just want him to be able to train for free?"

I could tell already that Coach didn't like this idea very much! But I kept trying! "That is the idea, Coach."

Coach got an understanding look on his face, and I thought maybe we had a chance, but then he said, "Listen, Marc. I understand that he doesn't have much money and that you are trying to help him, and that is really nice of you. But don't forget that I still have to pay rent for this building. I have to pay for insurance. I have to pay for any repairs that need to be done to the building. And I have to pay people to clean the place up: the mats, the locker rooms, and the bathrooms—everything. And on top of all that, don't forget that I have to have money to pay for my own house and my car and food for my wife and my baby daughter. And what happens when other people find out that I let some people train here for free? What will they think? Maybe they'll all start asking if they can train for free, too. And then what I am supposed to do? Is that fair? I don't think so. Your friend Nathan might not be able to afford to pay for classes, but I can't afford not to have him pay. I'm sorry, Marc, as much as I would like to help, nothing in life is free."

"Okay, Coach. Thanks for listening."

I walked over to Uncle Jake. "How'd it go?" he asked.

"Not good," I told him and then explained everything that coach had just told me. I was telling him about the rent, the repairs, and the cleaning, and when I got to the cleaning, he said, "Wait. Cleaning?"

"Yes, Uncle Jake. Someone has to clean up here every day. The mats. The locker rooms. The bathrooms. You know, all this stuff," I said.

"Good. That is the way."

"What way?" I asked.

"That is the way you can get Nathan to be able to train here. Not for free but by working. By cleaning."

"Oh yeah!" I said to Uncle Jake, realizing that was a great idea.

"But Coach also has a great point. All this stuff costs money. Lots of money. You have got to try and help there as well. How much money did you bring?"

"About two hundred dollars."

"Is that all of your money?"

"Yep, that's all of it." I really hoped Uncle Jake wasn't going to make me give up *all* my money.

"Okay. First, you need to save twenty percent of it. That's forty dollars. That leaves you one hundred sixty dollars. How much of that do you need?"

"Well, I'm not sure, Uncle Jake. I worked hard for that money."

Do you have any idea the mess you made?

Sup?

"I know you did," he told me. "And you should definitely keep a lot of it. But like I told you the other day, when it comes to money, the only feeling that compares to earning it is being able to use it to help someone else. What if you offer coach sixty dollars? And I said I will match what you put in. So your sixty plus another sixty from me comes to a total of one hundred twenty dollars. Plus, tell him you will clean the mats, the locker room, and the bathroom after every class."

"Okay, Uncle Jake," I told him. And I have to admit, even though I was feeling pretty bad about giving away sixty dollars, at the same time it also felt REALLY good to know I was going to be helping someone out.

I walked back over to Coach Adam. "Coach?"

"Yes, Marc?"

"My uncle Jake had an idea, and I wanted to see if you don't mind me asking for another way to have Nathan train here."

"Okay, Marc. Let's hear it."

"Well. First of all, I know nothing is free and that you have to work for everything. Luckily, I have been working hard all summer long mowing lawns and pulling weeds, and I've saved some money. I could give you sixty dollars. Plus my uncle wants to help out, too, so he said he would give the same amount as me, another sixty dollars. So that is a total of one hundred twenty dollars."

"That's really nice, Marc. And that's nice of your

uncle, too. But it costs a lot more than that to train here," Coach Adam said.

"I know. That's why we are going to offer to do more. We are going to clean the academy for you—Nathan and I. We will clean the mats, the locker rooms, the bathrooms . . . everything. We will do whatever else you need us to do around the outside of the academy, too. Pull weeds. Sweep up. We will keep this place in tip-top condition. It will be both of us cleaning, so we will do a great job. I promise."

Coach Adam sat for a minute, thinking. I could see he really wanted to help. But I still wasn't sure what he would say.

Finally, after what seemed like FOREVER, he said, "Okay."

At first, I didn't believe him. "Okay?"

"Yes, Marc. Okay. You can do it. You can bring

Nathan. He can train here. And you want to know why I am allowing it?"

"Because of the money?"

"No. Because of your attitude. One hundred twenty dollars isn't enough to cover many costs at all. And I won't save too much having you two clean. But your attitude is good. And because you and your uncle are trying to help, you are making me want to help, too. And that is part of jiu-jitsu, too. Being part of a team. Helping one another out. So if you give that money to help pay for things and you and Nathan help around here by cleaning up, then he can train here. Good job, Marc. Way to take care of your friend."

"Thank you, Coach!" I told him. Then we shook hands, and when we shook hands, it felt kinda different. Like when two adults shake hands. Like a business deal. It felt great spending money to help someone else. Uncle Jake was right!

I went over and told Uncle Jake that we had a deal. He got a big smile on his face, too. I went to the car and got my money and then Uncle Jake gave me his money, and I gave it all to Coach Adam.

When we got in the car, Uncle Jake said, "First mission accomplished. Good job, Marc."

"Thanks, Uncle Jake," I told him.

"Now we are on to mission number two."

"Mission number two? What is that?"

"Well, you wanted Nathan to be able to train in jiu-jitsu, but you also wanted him to get a bike. So we are going to get a bike."

After a few minutes, we pulled off the road by a sign that said JUNKYARD.

"Junkyard?" I asked. "We are going to look for a bike at the junkyard?"

"Yes, we sure are. People waste all kinds of stuff all the time. They throw away things that would work fine with a little time and effort."

We parked the car and got out. An older man wearing overalls walked over to us. "Good afternoon, folks. Whatcha lookin' for?"

"Good afternoon," said Uncle Jake, "we are looking for bikes."

"Okay, then. Second path over there, to the right.

Next to the appliances, just after the lawn furniture."

"Thank you, sir," Uncle Jake said as we headed down the second path.

We walked for a bit and finally walked past all the lawn furniture. Then I saw a HEAP of old bikes. Some were almost completely destroyed, but some of them weren't too bad. Some of them were even in better shape than The Bruiser was when we started working on it.

We climbed through and over the bikes, looking for one that was a kind of bike Nathan might like and wasn't in too horrible of shape.

As we were looking, our eyes both locked on one bike at the same time. It was a bluish color without too much rust. But the tires were flat, the handlebars were flipped upside down, it was missing one pedal, there were no grips on it, and overall, it just looked pretty rough. But not *too* rough. I looked at Uncle Jake, and he looked at me. We both smiled. It was the one!

We untangled it from some of the other bikes, and Uncle Jake carried it over to the man who had welcomed us.

"How much for this one?" Uncle Jake asked.

"How about two dollars?" the man said.

Two dollars! I thought to myself. The Bentlee cost almost TWO HUNDRED DOLLARS!

I reached into my pocket and pulled out two dollars. Uncle Jake took one of my dollars, then pulled out one of his own, and handed the money to the man.

"Looks like you got yourself a new bike! Well, maybe not a brand-new bike. But you got a bike."

"This kid will make it new," Uncle Jake said as he nodded at me.

"Well, good luck, kid," said the old man. "Good luck with that."

"Thank you, sir," I said. "I will do my best."

With that, we loaded the bike into the minivan and drove away.

"What was the last problem you wanted to help Nathan with?" Uncle Jake asked me.

"Well, I was hoping he could have a place to hang out after camp every day."

"That's right. And now he can help you get this bike fixed up. So now he will have a place to hang out—your garage—and he will have something to do while he is there—fixing this bike!"

"This is AWESOME, Uncle Jake," I said.

And I meant it. It was exactly as Uncle Jake had said it would be. Helping people helps everyone. I felt better already.

CHAPTER 21: A GREAT DAY

Today was one of the best days I've ever had. It started as soon as we got done with camp. I asked Nathan if he wanted to come over because I had some cool stuff for him.

"What kind of cool stuff?" he asked.

"Cool stuff. Trust me."

"Okay. Sounds good."

When camp was over, we headed back to my house. Since Nathan didn't have a bike, we took turns riding mine. I would ride for a block and he would run, then he would ride for a block and I would run. When we finally got to my house, we went around to the garage. I opened the garage and said, "There it is!"

"What?" Nathan said.

"That," I said as I pointed to the old blue bike that was sitting in the middle of the garage.

"That?" Nathan asked.

"Yes. That."

"An old bike?"

"Yes," I told him, "an old bike. But it's your bike. And I have all the tools and paint and gear to get it fixed up to be AWESOME."

Nathan stood there quietly for few moments with a look on his face like he couldn't believe it.

"Are you sure? For me?"

"Yep. It isn't ready to ride right now. But it will be. It looks about the same as The Bruiser looked when I first started fixing it."

"How long will it take to get ready?"

"It depends on how hard we work! I did most of the work last time by myself. With you here, it should go quicker. And I kinda know what I'm doing this time, which should also make it go even faster."

"Well, I am ready to work! Let's GO!"

When he said that, we got to WORK!

We did the same thing that I had done with The Bruiser:
We took off the wheels, the brakes, the handlebars, the
seat, the stem, the forks—EVERYTHING. It was cool having
Nathan there, and I could tell he really liked working on
the bike and learning all the different parts, and we
were having tons of fun as we did it. It was kind of hard
to believe that just a couple months ago, this was the
same kid who annoyed me like crazy and got me kicked
out of school on the last day!

After we had been there for a few hours, Uncle Jake
walked into the garage. "How is it going, boys?"

"It's going great, Uncle Jake!" Nathan said loudly.
Then he got quiet and said, "Sorry. I know you're not my
uncle."

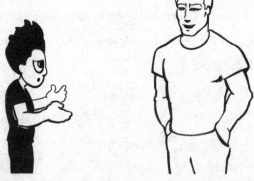

"That's all right, Nathan. You can call me Uncle Jake.
I don't mind one bit."

Nathan smiled. "Well, it is coming along great. We've
got the whole thing taken apart," Nathan said. "All the

pieces are organized in piles like the way you showed Marc last time."

"Yep! It is all squared away, Uncle Jake!" I added, pointing to the neat piles of bike parts.

"I see. You guys have done some great work. But now it's time for me to take you to jiu-jitsu," Uncle Jake said.

"Okay," I replied. I looked over at Nathan's face. I could see he was let down because he didn't think he could go.

"Well, I can just head home I guess. Thanks for having me over," Nathan said.

"Nope. You're coming with us," I told him.

"I can't," he said quietly. "I already used my one free class."

"I know you already used your free class. But remember today when I said I had some cool stuff for you?" I asked Nathan.

"Yeah, I remember."

"Well, this is the other cool thing. Jiu-jitsu."

"What about it?" Nathan asked.

"You can train there now! Whenever you want!"

"Wait. What? How?"

"Well, I know you really liked training there the other day. And Coach Adam noticed that you liked it a lot, too. And since I had a little extra money from working and

Uncle Jake always wants kids to learn jiu-jitsu, we were able to get a really good deal for your membership."

"I'm a member?" Nathan said, sounding thrilled. "AWESOME! THANK YOU!"

"Well, there is a little catch," I told him.

All of a sudden Nathan looked very serious, like maybe it was too good to be true.

"What is the catch?" he asked.

"Well. Since I couldn't pay the full price for the membership, I told Coach Adam that we would clean the mats, the bathrooms, the locker rooms . . . pretty much everything to pay for your training."

Nathan looked surprised. "That's it?" he asked. "That's the catch?! That's AWESOME! YES! We have jobs! At a jiu-jitsu academy! AAAWWWWEEESSSSOOOOMMMMEEEE!!!"

And that was it. We washed our hands (which were covered in dirt and grease and rust from taking apart the bike), grabbed a couple of my jiu-jitsu gis, and headed to the academy.

When we got there, we were a little early. Coach Adam had us sweep the floor and take out the garbage from all the different trash cans before class. He was really cool, and we were HAPPY TO BE THERE.

Then the class started. We warmed up and learned some moves and then it was time to train. I practiced a few moves, then Coach Adam put me into the "Shark Tank." The Shark Tank is what Coach Adam does to you when you are getting ready to compete. During the Shark Tank, I had to stay in the middle of the mat, grappling against the other kids one at a time. About every minute, Coach would send in a fresh person who was not tired at all. After about five minutes, I was really tired. After ten minutes, I was exhausted. And after fifteen minutes, I thought I was going to pass out—but I saw Uncle Jake was watching and thought, *NO WAY!*

I'd rather not fight that guy.

I stayed in there the whole time, giving it my best effort. There were even some people—kids who normally don't beat me—who were able to tap me out because I was so tired. Even a little girl named Zisa who is much smaller than me was able to tap me out with an armlock! But Coach said that was okay, because I kept trying my best. I kept moving as much as I could. By the time it was over, I could barely stand up.

But I did stand up. I shook everyone's hand, and Coach Adam said, "Nice work, Marc. As long as you fight that hard in the tournament, I will be happy."

"I will, Coach. I will."

And with that, Nathan and I walked off the mat to where Uncle Jake was waiting. I was sweating. HARD.

If someone wants to call a medic, I wouldn't argue. . . .

We got in the car, and Uncle Jake started driving. I was too tired to talk, so I was just kind of sitting there. Then Nathan said, "That was cool to watch, Marc. You did awesome."

"Thanks, Nathan," I said.

He was quiet for a little while. Then he said, "No, Marc. Thank you. And you, too, Uncle Jake. Thank both of you. For everything."

And with that, we drove back to the house, tired, sweaty, and happy.

It was a great day.

CHAPTER 22: WIN OR LEARN

So. Today I participated in my first jiu-jitsu tournament. It was CRAZY!

I have to admit that it was even harder than I thought it would be. First of all, the scene was nuts. The crowd was berserk. I have never been around so many people yelling and screaming so much. And it was HARD. The kids I fought against were GOOD and STRONG.

Before my first match, I was super nervous. The kid was named Barry, and he was bigger than me. When I walked out onto the mat, I actually felt like I was going to throw up! The referee had us shake hands, then bow, and then he said, "Fight!"

When he grabbed my gi, I could already feel something different than what it felt like in training. He was grabbing me HARD! He pulled me and pushed me and pulled me and pushed me, and I felt like he was going to throw me across the mat! Then he stepped in and tripped me to the ground, but luckily I was able to put him in the guard on my way down. Once we were on the ground, I realized once again how crazy competition actually was! He was going nuts! I kept my guard closed tight and tried to pull him down and control him. Then he grabbed the collar of my gi and started trying to choke me. At first, I started to panic as it got harder to breath. Then I heard Coach Adam say calmly, "Relax and do what you know how to do."

At first, I thought, *IT IS A LITTLE HARD TO RELAX WHEN SOMEONE IS TRYING TO CHOKE ME!!!!* Then I thought, *Just listen to Coach.* So I did. I tried to relax and detach from all the emotion and chaos of the fight. Suddenly I felt much better. I thought about what I knew how to do. Then it hit me: ARMLOCK! This was the perfect spot to do an ARMLOCK. His arm was straightened out as he tried to choke me, all I had to do was lock his arm into position with my legs and use my hips to put pressure on his

arm. So I did it! I swung my legs around his arm and trapped it and moved my hips to apply the force, and HE TAPPED OUT! HE TAPPED OUT!

I looked over and saw Nathan jump in the air, and Coach Adam nodded his head and mouthed the words *Good job.*

Uncle Jake was standing on the sideline with a MASSIVE smile on his face as he pumped his fist. I WON MY FIRST JIU-JITSU MATCH.

But that was only the beginning. As soon as I walked off the mat, Coach Adam said, "Great work. Now relax and get ready for your next match."

NEXT MATCH??? I just finished my first match! I sat down and drank some water. Nathan came over to me. "That was AWESOME! YOU TAPPED HIM OUT!"

"Thanks! It was crazy!"

"What was crazy about it?" he asked.

"The whole thing. The crowd. The screaming. How hard my opponent was fighting. Everything."

"It might have been crazy, but you DID IT!"

"I guess so!" I said, still kind of not believing that it had happened.

"What's next?" Nathan asked in an excited voice.

"I have to get ready for the next match," I told him.

"Okay. Do you need anything from me?" Nathan asked.

"No. I'm okay. Thanks, though," I told him. I sat there, still trying to catch my breath.

Uncle Jake walked over toward me. "Relax," he said. "Just relax."

"I'm trying," I told him.

"I know," he said. "It's hard."

Then I heard Coach Adam say, "Marc, next match. Let's go!"

I got up and moved back over to where coach was. The referee pointed at me and waved me on to the mat. Here we go again! My second match and I was still tired from the first one!

The kid I was going against in this match was about the same size as me. He looked like he was at least as nervous as I was! But you never can tell what someone is going to be like on the mat until you *feel* what they are like on the mat. As it turns out, this kid was STRONG!

As soon as the ref said "Fight!" the kid's face turned from nervous to angry, and he charged at me and shot for my legs. He was trying the classic double-leg takedown, and I did the classic double-leg takedown defense: I sprawled, kicking my legs out behind me and landing with my chest on his back. I thought I had him stuck, but then he did something called a sit-out, which is great wrestling move, and it almost put me on my face. But I knew it was coming, so I scrambled away and got back to my feet. The kid looked like he was going crazy. Every time he grabbed me, he snuck in a little slap and then pinched my skin. Every time he touched me, it hurt—and it definitely seemed like he was doing it on purpose.

Then, as we approached each other again, both of us looking to score a takedown, he popped his head into my head with some force, head-butting me. That REALLY hurt. And that is when it started to happen. I didn't notice it at first—but I started getting mad. REALLY MAD. I started losing my temper. I could barely tell, but Uncle Jake could.

"Detach," he said from the side of the mat. "Don't get emotional. Do your job. Do what you know how to do." As soon as I heard Uncle Jake say that, I knew he was right—I was losing my temper. I was breathing harder and all my muscles were too tense, and it was making me out of breath. So despite my opponent slapping, pinching, and head-butting me every chance he got, I calmed down. I got my temper under control. And I think this frustrated my opponent even more—his face started turning redder and redder and redder and redder! His slaps got harder, and he charged forward like a bull. After another hard head-butt, I saw a look in his eyes of total rage. He shot in toward my legs to take me down again, but he made a classic mistake—he left his head sticking out. It was easy. I barely moved my arms and I had his neck trapped in a choke. I felt him panic and wiggle like crazy, trying to get me off of him. Then, finally, he tapped out. The referee placed his hands on us and said, "That's it." I let go of the choke and stood up. The referee pulled us to the middle of the mat and raised my hand. I had won.

"Next up is the finals, Marc," Coach Adam said to me.

"Okay" was all I could say—I was too tired! Even though I had stayed calm, it was still a TOUGH match and I was TIRED.

Uncle Jake came by and said, "Nice work again, Marc. You ready for the finals?"

"I am," I told Uncle Jake. And I felt that I was. Even though I was tired, I had been doing REALLY WELL! I felt like I could win this whole thing!

I sat for a few minutes and then they called my name again. I walked out onto the mat once more. "This is for the final," the referee said as I stood there facing my opponent. My opponent looked very calm. He was actually a little bit smaller than me, but I knew that skill level was more important than size and that for him to be in the finals, he must have some really good jiu-jitsu. We shook hands, and the referee pointed to us both, then clapped his hands and said, "Fight!"

I made my way to the center of the mat and so did

my opponent. We circled cautiously, then he grabbed my head and pulled it down toward the ground. I pulled my head back up, hard, to get away from him. He took another step toward me, then grabbed my head again and pulled it down even harder. So I pulled my head up even harder to prevent him from putting my face into the mat. When I did that, he let go of my head and quickly shot for my feet. My head, body, and arms were so high that he got right in and wrapped up my legs, then he hoisted me way into the air and slammed me to the mat with a perfect double-leg takedown. By the time I hit the ground, he was already across my side. As I moved to defend that, he was suddenly in the mount. I stayed calm and got into a defensive position. I felt him digging at the collar of my gi, trying to get a choke on me. But I wasn't having any of that! I pulled my arms in to defend my neck from his attack.

Then—BOOM! In a flash, he switched the attack from a choke to an armlock. Before I knew it, he had my arm completely straightened out and I was tapping. That was it. It was over.

I started to get mad, but I looked over at Uncle Jake. "Win, or learn," he said. "You learned." He was right. Seeing that Uncle Jake was perfectly calm calmed me down, too.

"I guess I learned from that one, Coach Adam," I said right after I shook my opponent's hand.

Then I sat down next to Nathan. "That was awesome!" he said.

"Awesome? What? The armlock he did?"

"No. This whole day. It was awesome. You're awesome."

"You think so?"

"I know so," he said. "That was so cool, the way you handled yourself out there. But not just out there. Everywhere. Your bike. Your job. Your attitude with everything. Where does all this come from?"

I thought about it for a minute. I sure had changed a lot from the kid that lost his temper and threw the papier-mâché pumpkin at Nathan. I had learned even more about being a warrior.

"It came from my uncle Jake. He taught me a lot. He taught me to be a Warrior Kid."

"A Warrior Kid?" Nathan asked. "What is that?"

"I'll tell you when we get back to my house."

With that, I got on the pedestal to receive my second-place medal and then headed home.

I had won something more important than second place today. I learned more about jiu-jitsu. I learned more about myself.

CHAPTER 23: THE CODE

When we got back to my house, I sat down and told Nathan EVERYTHING. I told him how I had been a really wimpy kid in fifth grade. That I couldn't swim, I couldn't do any pull-ups, that I didn't know my times tables, and that I was getting picked on by Kenny Williamson.

"I thought you and Kenny were friends?" Nathan asked.

"We are now," I told him, "but he used to bully me."

"So what happened? How did you go from being that wimpy kid to being who you are now?"

Now . . . we're practically besties.

"My uncle Jake trained me all last summer. We worked out every day. He taught me how to study. He taught me how to swim. He put me into jiu-jitsu classes. He even got me eating good foods!"

"Was it hard?"

"Of course it was. It still is. But I still stay on the path."

"What path?" Nathan asked.

"The path of being a Warrior Kid," I told him. "Following the code."

"The code?"

"Yes. The code. Warriors have codes that they follow. Not like secret codes but more like rules. It is called *discipline*."

"Discipline?"

"That's right. Discipline. *Discipline* means you follow the rules, not because someone else makes you follow them but because following the rules makes you a better person."

"So what are the rules?" Nathan asked.

I pulled out the Warrior Kid Code and showed it to him.

The Warrior Kid Code

1. The Warrior Kid wakes up early in the morning.
2. The Warrior Kid studies to learn and gain knowledge and asks questions if he doesn't understand.
3. The Warrior Kid trains hard, exercises, and eats right to be strong and fast and healthy.
4. The Warrior Kid trains to know how to fight so he can stand up to bullies to protect the weak.
5. The Warrior Kid treats people with respect and helps out other people whenever possible.
6. The Warrior Kid keeps things neat and is always prepared and ready for action.
7. The Warrior Kid stays humble.
8. The Warrior Kid works hard and always does his best.
9. I am the Warrior Kid.

Then I told him I was adding some stuff to it. "What are you adding?" he asked.

"Well," I said, "I'm glad you asked, because they are things that you helped teach me."

"I helped teach you? What did I help teach you?" Nathan asked.

I took out my pen, went to line number seven, and added to it so it said, *The Warrior Kid stays humble and stays calm. Warriors Kids do not lose their tempers.*

"When I threw that pumpkin at you and got in trouble at school—that was because I lost my temper. I didn't stay calm. When you lose your temper, you do stupid things. Warriors can't lose their tempers."

"What else are you adding to it?"

I moved my pen to number eight and made it read, *The Warrior Kid works hard, saves money, is frugal and doesn't waste things, and always does his best.*

"What is *frugal*?" Nathan asked.

"*Frugal* means you don't waste things," I told him.

"Why is that important to a warrior?" Nathan asked.

"Because warriors have to make things last and make things work. If a warrior is in the field, he might not have extra stuff. Not extra food, not extra gear, not extra time. So warriors try not to waste anything. I learned that by fixing my bike this summer. It seemed like junk, but it wasn't junk at all. It just needed to be taken care of. Warriors take care of their gear. They don't waste it. And saving money gives you freedom. It might not feel like it at first, because you want to buy a treat at the candy store or some little toy from the shop. But those are just a waste of money, and if you spend your money on those things, then you won't be able to buy anything that will really help you. But if you save your money, you'll have the freedom buy things that you REALLY want."

"That does make sense. The more you save, the more you are free."

"Yep. It is the same with everything. Discipline Equals Freedom. My uncle Jake taught that to me. The harder you work and the more you follow the rules you make for yourself, the more freedom you have. And that includes having the discipline to NOT throw pumpkins at kids in school!"

Nathan laughed.

"Now, speaking of bikes, we have got some work to do." And with that, we went down to the garage and got busy. We had cleaned and oiled and painted the parts, and now all that was left was to put them together. I had told Uncle Jake what we were doing, and he told me to come get him if we needed any help. But guess what? We didn't need any help at all! We put the whole bike back together by ourselves. By the time Uncle Jake came up from the house, it was ready.

"Dang!" Uncle Jake said. "That looks great!"

"Thanks, Uncle Jake," I said.

"What are you going to name it?" Uncle Jake asked Nathan.

"Name it?" Nathan asked.

"Yeah. You get to name it. Just like Marc got to name his bike The Bruiser, you get to name this bike. Here," Uncle Jake said as he reached into a drawer and pulled out the letter stickers .

Nathan took the stickers and said, "Okay. But I'm not sure what to name it."

"Well, it's up to you, so you better think of something," Uncle Jake said.

Nathan sat there for a minute. Then he said, "How about 'The Discipline'?"

"I like it," Uncle Jake said, "but why?"

"Well, because without discipline, this bike wouldn't be here. Marc wouldn't have had the money to buy it. Without discipline, we wouldn't have taken the time to fix it up. It would still be in the junkyard. But now it is free to ride again. It is free because of discipline. So we will call it The Discipline."

"Right on!" I declared, thinking how cool that sounded.

"Sounds like you are on the right path, Nathan."

"He is, Uncle Jake."

"I am, Uncle Jake," Nathan said. "I'm on the path to be a Warrior Kid."

"Yes, you are, Nathan. Yes, you are."

With that, Uncle Jake handed Nathan the bag of stickers and we spelled out THE DISCIPLINE on the side of his bike. It looked COOL. Then Uncle Jake opened the garage door, and we took the bikes for a spin around the block, down the road, and through the park.

We were free.

CHAPTER 24: THE LEADER

The next day, Nathan came over and actually copied down the Warrior Kid Code word for word. He asked questions about working out and how to study. We even made some flash cards for some vocabulary words that we were supposed to learn over the summer.

The last week of camp was great. We did all kinds of cool projects and sports, and the camp counselors even let me show some basics of jiu-jitsu to the class. It was AWESOME.

Then, suddenly, on Sunday morning, it was time for Uncle Jake to head back to college.

We did one more workout together early in the morning—this time we did two hundred pull-ups! It was crazy. It was even crazier that in the beginning of last summer, I couldn't even do ONE!

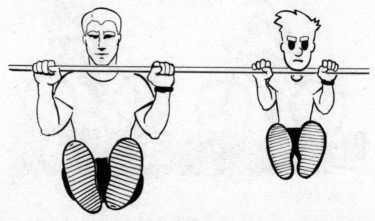

Once we were done working out, Uncle Jake sat in my room while I was cleaning up.

"So what did you learn this summer?" he asked.

"A ton!" I said.

"Like what?" he asked again.

"Well. I learned to control my temper!" I said with a smile.

"Yes. You learned about that. What else?"

"I learned about taking care of my gear. And that includes how to completely break down and refurbish a bike .... or two bikes, to be exact."

"Ah yes. That is a good lesson, too. What else?" Uncle Jake asked.

"I learned about hard work and business and how to be frugal and save my money."

"Yes. That's true. And very important. But what else did you learn?"

"That jiu-jitsu tournaments are nothing to be afraid of? And that I'm actually pretty good at them?"

"Yes, Marc, you learned that, too. But what else?"

I wasn't quite sure what Uncle Jake was getting at. "I learned not to let things like name-calling bother me. And how to take the power away from an insult by simply laughing at it?"

"Yes, Marc, you learned that, too. But you're missing the most important lesson from the summer."

I racked my brain but couldn't think of anything, so I told Uncle Jake, "I'm not sure. Can you tell me?"

FEEL FREE TO GIVE ME A CLUE.

"Okay," he said, "let me give you a hint. What do you think about Nathan?"

"What about Nathan? I think he's a great kid. I like him a lot."

"Did you like him before?"

"No. I didn't."

"Why not?" Uncle Jake asked.

"Well, because he was kind of a jerk."

"What changed him?"

I wasn't sure what Uncle Jake meant by this. "What changed him?" I asked him back.

"Yes," he said again, "what changed him? What made him start acting nice? What put him on the path to being a Warrior Kid?"

I thought about it for a while and then I thought I realized what Uncle Jake was getting at.

"Was . . . it . . . me?" I asked nervously.

Uncle Jake nodded his head. "Yes, yes it was you. That is the biggest lesson of the summer. You learned to lead—and you learned the power of being a leader. Your positive influence on Nathan will impact his whole life. Everything. And that is what a leader does. A leader helps people without expecting anything in return. And that's what you did, Marc. You led Nathan down the right path—the warrior path—and you did it for him—not for you. I'm proud of you Marc. Because that's what warriors do. Warriors lead."

I walked back over to my Warrior Kid Code, which I had sitting on my desk. I read through it again. Line nine, which said *I am the Warrior Kid*, seemed to be missing something. I picked a pen up off the desk and added *and I am a leader* to that line.

I held it up and showed it to Uncle Jake.

He nodded his head. "Perfect," he said. "You are a leader."

"Yes, I am," I said.

Uncle Jake packed up the last of his gear, and we headed to the airport. We didn't say much on the way there. My mom asked some questions about classes he would be taking, and he talked through some of them.

I was sad once again that Uncle Jake was leaving. But at the same time, I felt good, though I wasn't quite sure why.

When we got to the airport, we got out of the car and I went to say good-bye to him. He looked me square in the eye. "It feels good, doesn't it?" he asked.

"What?" I said, wondering how he could tell what I was feeling.

"It feels good to lead people down the path. I led you down the path last year. Now you led Nathan. And you will lead others, Marc. That is your new mission: You will lead others."

"I will, Uncle Jake. I will."

And with that, he shook my hand and headed toward the terminal to catch his plane.

My leader was gone.

But it didn't matter as much this time.

Because I was the leader now.

The Warrior Kid Code

1. The Warrior Kid wakes up early in the morning.

2. The Warrior Kid studies to learn and gain knowledge and asks questions if he doesn't understand.

3. The Warrior Kid trains hard, exercises, and eats right to be strong and fast and healthy.

4. The Warrior Kid trains to know how to fight so he can stand up to bullies to protect the weak.

5. The Warrior Kid treats people with respect and helps out other people whenever possible.

6. The Warrior Kid keeps things neat and is always prepared and ready for action.

7. The Warrior Kid stays humble.

8. The Warrior Kid works hard and always does his best.

9. I am the Warrior Kid and I am a leader.

Turn the page for a look at the first book
in the Way of the Warrior Kid series!

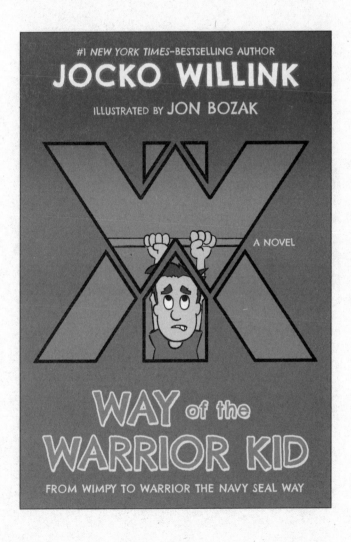

CHAPTER 1: THE WORST YEAR

Tomorrow is the last day of school, and I CAN'T WAIT FOR IT TO BE OVER!! This has been the worst year EVER! The bad part is that I don't see how next year is going to be any better at all. Fifth grade was horrible—I'm afraid sixth grade will be EVEN WORSE. Why was it so bad? Where do I begin?

This is ME (Marc).

I'm the hot dog-eating champ in my house!

This guy can beat me in a foot race.

Top five reasons why fifth grade was HORRIBLE:

1. It's school! I'm sitting at a desk ALL DAY.
2. I learned that I'm dumb! That's right. All the other grades I thought I was "smart." But this year was a FAILURE! I still don't know my times tables! How the heck am I going to make it through next year?

3. School lunches. They call it "pizza." I have no idea why. Since when does a piece of white bread count as pizza crust???????

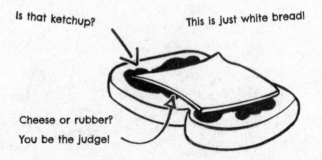

Is that ketchup?

This is just white bread!

Cheese or rubber?
You be the judge!

4. Gym class. Most people like gym. But at my school we have "tests" and I completely stink. Especially at PULL-UPS. Guess how many pull-ups I can do? ZERO! I can do ZERO pull-ups! I'm a disgrace to ten-year-olds—and the whole class knows it. Even the girls. Especially the girls that can do more pull-ups than me!!

I did one pull-up. How many can you do?

I try not to define my efforts with numbers.

5. Field trips. Just like gym class, most kids like field trips. Well, we go to one place for field trips: Mount Tom. We go there in the fall before it gets too cold and in the spring when it starts to get warm. But here's the thing: Mount Tom isn't a mountain. It's a lake. Here's the problem: I CAN'T SWIM! I hid it pretty well during our fall trip. But this spring,

kids noticed. "Why don't you come out in the water?" "Why are you staying on the beach?" "Why don't you jump off the diving board?" What kind of person can't even swim? ME: That's what kind of person! AAAHHH!

6. I know I said top five reasons, but there is one more, and it's probably the biggest reason: Kenny Williamson. He is big and he is MEAN. He rules the jungle gym. He even calls himself "King of the Jungle Gym" or "King Kenny"!! If any other kids want to play on the jungle gym, they either have to be friends with Kenny or follow his "rules."

These things could hurt someone!

A HUMAN TIME BOMB!

All the teachers talk about how my school is "bully-free." We even had a No Bully Day, where we talked about bullying and how bad it was and how we should tell the teachers if we saw it happening. Well, let me tell you, Kenny is definitely a BULLY, and he definitely is in my school. And no one says anything to the teachers about it!

Those are the top reasons that fifth grade was horrible, and sixth grade isn't going to be much better! I can't wait for school to be over tomorrow so the suffering can STOP and summer can START!

This summer is going to be AWESOME. Yes, it is cool that I won't have to be in school—but something even cooler is happening. My uncle Jake is coming to stay with us for the whole summer!

He has been a Navy SEAL for eight years and is getting out of the Navy to go to college. Before he goes to college, he is going to stay with us the whole summer long. A Navy SEAL! FOR REAL. IN MY HOUSE!!!!!

Uncle Jake is the best. First, he is super cool because he is a Navy SEAL. He fought in real wars. My mom says he was "on the front lines." That means he was face-to-face with the bad guys. Whoa! Uncle Jake is also awesome because he is the COMPLETE OPPOSITE OF ME. I am weak—he is strong. I am dumb—he is smart. I can't swim—he can swim with a backpack on! I'm scared of bullies—bullies are scared of him!

MY UNCLE JAKE!!

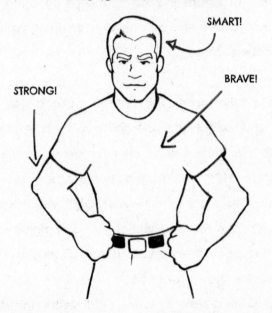

SMART!

BRAVE!

STRONG!

Anyway, I haven't spent too much time with Uncle Jake because we live in California, and he has been stationed in Virginia for a long time. I hope he doesn't think I'm such a DUMB WIMP that he won't even hang around with me! Maybe he won't notice?

AAHHHHH!!! Of course he will. He is a tough guy! I'm a dork! Well, I guess I will find out soon.